Elizab_____New Zealand and moved to England with her family when she was three. She went to school in Croydon, studied languages at Bristol and then Edinburgh University, and taught English in Malaysia, Ethiopia and India. She has written many books for children, including the *Wild Things* series, *Kiss the Dust* (winner of the Children's Book Award) and *Secret Friends* (nominated for the Carnegie Medal). Her novel *Red Sky in the Morning* was Highly Recommended for the Carnegie Medal and shortlisted for the 1989 Children's Book Award. *Jake's Tower* was shortlisted for the 2001 Carnegie Medal and the Guardian Children's Book Award 2001. She lives with her husband on the edge of Richmond Park in Surrey.

'Splendid and moving, *Jake's Tower*, the story of a boy bullied and beaten by his mother's boyfriend, has great emotional power and insight'
*East Anglian Daily Times*

*Also by Elizabeth Laird*

The *Wild Things* series

*Red Sky in the Morning*
*Kiss the Dust*
*Secret Friends*
*Hiding Out*
*Jay*
*Forbidden Ground*
*When the World Began:*
*Stories Collected in Ethiopia*

# Jake's Tower

### Elizabeth Laird

MACMILLAN CHILDREN'S BOOKS

*For Jane Fior*

First published 2001 by Macmillan Children's Books
This edition published 2002 by Macmillan Children's Books
a division of Macmillan Publishers Limited
20 New Wharf Road, London N1 9RR
Basingstoke and Oxford
www.panmacmillan.com

Associated companies throughout the world

ISBN 0 330 39803 2

5 7 9 8 6

A CIP catalogue record for this book is available from
the British Library.

Phototypeset by Intype London Ltd
Printed and bound in Great Britain by
Mackays of Chatham plc, Chatham, Kent.

I found a secret place today. It was by accident. I was racing out of the house, running as fast as I could, anything to get away, and I got through the hole in the fence at the end of the lane, just above the railway line.

I wriggled through the bushes, and then I fell into it. Right in. Splat.

It's a good place. There are two huge square blocks, chunks of concrete, with a bit of space between. Not more than a metre and a half, I'd say. The blocks must have been there for ages because plants and creepers have grown up all over and round them. The creepers stretch over between the blocks to make a kind of roof. Once I've crawled inside it's like being in a little house. My house.

I could clean this place up and make it better. I could get a bit of plastic sheeting to put under the creepers to make a watertight roof. I could sleep here then if I had to. If it comes to that.

I'd get started today if I could, but I can't do much because of my arm. The bruise is going to be the biggest I've ever had, I think. I'm not sure. It's hard to tell with bruises.

The one on my back after Christmas might have been bigger, but you can't tell when they're on your back because you can't see them properly. This one's

1

coming up blue now, then it'll go purple with yellow bits in it. He never does them on my face in case someone sees.

The bruise is on my right arm, but I can do things with my left. I can pick things up. I could pick up sticks and things if I wanted to, but I don't. Not today.

She used to shout at him when he got going, when things started to get really bad. She doesn't now. She doesn't look at my bruises, either. She just goes quiet if she sees them, and her eyes slide away.

It's like when you smell something bad and you turn your head away because you don't want to know about it.

I get scared, often, in case it's not my bruises that make her look away. In case it's me. That's why I don't say much in front of her any more. I don't show her what he's done to me.

It's good that I've found this place. I can come here and make my plans. I can do my thinking in here, and be safe.

My main plan for the future is my dream house. It's going to be very tall and thin, a tower, really. There's going to be a moat all the way around it, and the only way over it is by a drawbridge that's pulled up all the time, except when I want to get across myself.

There'll be a lift in the tower to whiz me up to the top. My room will be up there. It's totally safe. There's no way anyone can get to me. No way at all.

There'll be a window with a lookout place on it, like a balcony. I'll have a telescope out there, on the balcony, and I'll be able to see for miles and miles.

Keep a check to see if anyone's coming near, in case I have to take precautions. And just in case, just supposing I need it, I'll have one of those huge, great balloons tied up to the balcony, the ones you can go in, with a basket underneath. And if I really have to, I'll get in the basket, and untie the rope, and float away. No one could get me then.

But I wouldn't ever need to. I wouldn't have to worry, because of the moat and the drawbridge. And even if he did get across somehow, I'd fix it so the lift wouldn't go down for him. It would be my lift, just obeying me. Voice activated, or something.

'Little bastard', he called me, when he pulled me out from under my bed this morning. 'Dirty, sneaky, snivelling little rat.'

I wouldn't even hear him in my tower, however loud he shouted. I'd just be too high up.

A bird was singing in the lane when I came back from my secret place today.

I don't worry about that kind of thing usually, but the song went right through me. Directly into my head. I looked up, and there he was, sitting on the top of the tallest tree, and I thought, Good for you. You're all right up there.

Maybe I was there too long, though, looking up into the tree. I should have looked round anyway, before I dived in through the hole in the fence, to make sure no one was there. But I didn't, and there was someone. He was a boy from my school.

I saw him too late, when I'd already bent down. I moved back again, of course. Pretended I'd only been looking at something through the chain link, but he gave me a funny look. I think he knew that I was hiding something. He must have known. He'll have worked out that there was a hole in the fence, and he'll know I was about to go in there.

What if he does a bit of snooping round? What if he comes in here and finds my secret place?

There's a spider in here. A really big one. I don't mind him. He doesn't bother me, and I don't bother him. I quite like him, actually, because he's making a gigantic web. He'd done all the spokes out from the middle before I got here and now he's filling it in with the cross pieces. Backwards and forwards he goes.

I've been watching the spider and thinking about Kieran. That's the name of the boy I saw just now. He's in one of the other classes in my year, so I don't know him very well. I'm not sure what he's like, if he's one of those teasing ones, or a quiet sort of person like me.

I don't know if spiders make good pets. You couldn't tame them, I shouldn't think, and they're not exactly cuddly, are they? Not like Paws. She was good, my guinea pig was. Her nose twitched and she was warm. The softest thing you could imagine.

He should never have done that, picking up her cage and throwing it out of the door. I thought she was OK. She seemed it, that day and the day after, but the day after that she was dead. Stiff and cold and looking small, as if she'd shrunk or something. Paws.

'Don't you bring all your dirty animals in here again,' he said, and when I couldn't stop crying he belted me so hard I fell on to the table and broke my arm.

'Playing football,' she said to the doctor, when she took me off to Casualty. 'You know what boys are like at that age.'

But on the way home from the hospital, she bought me a bag of sweets, and we sat on the top of the bus, and she put her arm round me, carefully, so as not to hurt mine, and she cried and cried (a good thing the bus was empty), and said she was sorry, and she'd never let him touch me again. I cried too, as a matter of fact.

School doesn't bother me most of the time. I just go there and do what I'm supposed to do and mind my own business. Keep myself to myself. Mrs McLeish doesn't notice me if I'm quiet and sit at the back. I don't listen half the time, except sometimes, like the other day, when she was reading a poem.

I learned the last bit straight off. She didn't need to say it twice.

> *'The silver apples of the moon.*
> *The golden apples of the sun.'*

I don't know what it means, but it doesn't matter. I just like the words. That poem made me think that maybe I ought to have a bit of garden round my tower house. The moat would make it like a sort of island, and I could make the whole thing bigger and plant some trees in it.

Not big trees. Not so that he could climb up them and get to my balcony. Just little ones with fruit on them. Silver apples shining in the night and golden apples for the day. Nice to eat too, more like peaches than apples, with juice that runs everywhere.

Just for me. And maybe for the spider.

A train's coming. I can see the people as clear as anything as it goes past. They can't see me, though, hidden in my secret place. I can sit here and look out and watch the world go by.

That's what I like best. I'm safe and no one can see me. I can watch the world go by.

She's going to have a baby! She didn't tell me herself. I found out because I heard them after I'd gone to bed. She was crying.

'I don't want this sodding baby!' she kept saying. 'I'm going to get rid of it. You can't stop me.'

I didn't want to hear her saying that. I stuck my head under the cover and tried to think about my silver apple tree, but I couldn't help listening.

He was being really nice to her, the way he is sometimes. The way he is even to me, sometimes.

'No,' he kept saying, all soft and sweet. 'Come on. You don't mean that. Think of it, Marie, a little baby! We'll be a proper family. It's all I ever wanted, a family of my own, like I never had.'

'You'll go for him,' she said, 'like you go for Jake. Look how you broke his arm. I should have chucked you out straight away for that. And for what you do to me.'

His voice went so low I couldn't hear what he said next, except for a few words.

'My temper,' he said. 'Don't know what comes over me. I promise. Never again.'

A baby! Could be a boy or a girl. A brother or a sister.

It made me scared, though, the thought of a baby.

6

Scared me to death. I was so scared I got out of bed, even though I know the floorboards creak. If he hears me move around after I'm supposed to be in bed, he's in my room like a flash beating the daylights out of me. But I needed something.

OK, I know it's soft, a boy of my age wanting a baby's toy, especially when its beak started coming off years ago, and one of its feet is lost. But I did want it. I keep Ducky hidden most of the time so he won't find it. If he did he'd sneer at me and throw it out. So I only fetch Ducky out from the back of my drawer when I really, really need him.

I managed it all right. I crossed the room, opened the drawer, got Ducky out, shut the drawer and started back. I had to freeze halfway to my bed, because their voices suddenly stopped, and I thought he must be about to roar in and grab Ducky and murder me, but they went on talking after a bit. I was shaking from head to foot.

'It's OK, Ducky,' I kept whispering. 'I won't let him hurt you.'

And then I thought, I'll be saying that to a real live baby soon, and the scared feeling got so bad I started shivering all over, and when I got into bed I squeezed poor old Ducky so tight I was afraid his stuffing would pop out.

She never talks about my dad.

'He was only sixteen,' she says, if ever I ask. 'Who knows anything about anything when they're only sixteen?'

She's wrong about that. I won't be sixteen for

years and years, but I know more than I want to already.

'So what happened to him, then?' I say, pressing her a bit.

'I've told you a dozen times. He joined up, didn't he? Went into the army. Got sent off abroad somewhere. And there's no use your asking me where, because I don't know, and anyway it wouldn't do you any good because he's got another family now.'

I don't like it when she says that, but I go on anyway.

'What do you mean, another family? How many kids?'

She gets mad at me then.

'How should I know? I haven't seen him since the day you were born.'

'Tell me about it. Go on, Mum. Please.'

'I've told you, hundreds of times. He came into the ward—'

'Did he look at me straight off, or later?'

'Then. Straight off. He put that fluffy duck into your cot. Then he says his mum's made him promise he won't see me any more, and he didn't mean for it to happen, and we'd split up before I even knew I was pregnant, and anyway he was off to become a soldier.'

'Then he picked me up and gave me a cuddle.'

'Yes, he did. Looked as if he was going to start crying, and rushed off. That's all. You know it is.'

'No. You've left out the letter.'

'What letter? Oh, that. When you were six. It came from Germany. Jake, give over. I've told you all this, hundreds of times.'

'Tell me again, then.'

'He wrote and said he thought about you a lot—'

'All the time, that's what he said.'

'And he wanted to know about you, and he'd got a wife, and a baby on the way and he wanted me to write and tell him how you were.'

'So you did.'

'Yes, I bloody well did. Asked him for some money too, the cheeky sod. They earn a fortune in the army.'

'But he didn't write back.'

'No. He didn't write back.'

I think I might have a special place on my island for my dad, in case he ever comes to see me. He might. It could happen.

He must know where to find us because of the letters. He sent his to her in a roundabout way through someone they'd known at school. They both grew up in this town, though he lived on the other side, I think. She never said.

My dad's room will be at the bottom of the tower. It ought to be the kind of place soldiers like, with a couple of crossed flags stuck up on the wall and a few old guns on wheels like in the castle we went to on our school trip last term.

Maybe he wouldn't like that, though. Maybe he's fed up with the army. I think he must be, because I'm sure I'm like him and the army wouldn't do for me at all. No way. Not in a month of Sundays. Being a soldier means being yelled at all the time, and put in the glasshouse when there's a fight. And you have to be ready to kill people. I don't want to kill anyone or hurt anyone. Not ever.

My dad's room will be very nice, with two really comfortable chairs, one for him and one for me, and a massive TV, and shelves stacked with videos, and a cupboard between us with a little handset thing you can press to make whatever you want to eat or drink pop up. You want crisps? You just press the crisp logo and out shoots a bag of crisps. He'd really like that.

There'd be a big window on one side, that you could slide back so that you could smell the silver and golden apple trees outside. Because they'd have a wonderful smell, like a perfume, the best you've ever smelled. And the apples would spin like strobes and the sparkly light would flash into the room and make everything look as if it was dancing.

He won't want to be a slob all the time, though, my dad won't, because he's really fit, being a soldier, so I'd better have a football place where we can play football together. I'd have to make the island bigger, but I could do that. Push it out beyond the apple trees. We'd have a proper goal, why not? and take it in turns to shoot.

He'd be brilliant at it and he'd give me loads of tips and I'd get brilliant at it too.

I don't suppose he'd want to come all that often to my island as he's got this other kid, and maybe more by now. They wouldn't be allowed to come. Not till I got to know them, anyway.

I'd keep a lookout from my tower for my dad. It could work on an infra-red system, picking up his shape. Or perhaps he'd have a remote control thing in his pocket to warn me he was coming. The minute

I got the signal, I'd whiz down from my tower in the lift, and let the drawbridge down for him.

I wouldn't have to be in my tower at all while he was on the island, because he'd protect me if Steve came. He wouldn't let Steve come anywhere near.

Steve would be terrified of my dad. His face would go white and his voice would croak and his heart would thump and his hands would go wet and his knees would knock just like mine do when he starts to go for me. He'd turn round and make a dash for it.

You wouldn't see him for dust. He'd be over the hills and far away. He'd be out of it, and good riddance. That's what would happen if Steve tried to get on to my island when my dad was there.

In the army they have to bivouac when they get stuck out in the open and can't get back in for the night. I saw a programme about it. They dig holes in the ground and get in there. Foxholes, they call them. They put branches over the top for camouflage and then they get in and hide inside.

Usually there's two people in a foxhole, but I don't want anyone else in mine. No way.

I wouldn't fight anyone who came. I'd just go away and plan how to get them out. I'd wait till they'd gone, then come back in myself. I'm patient. That's my way. Cunning.

If Kieran comes through the fence and pokes around here he'll find my secret place at once. He'll get through the hole and walk down the path my feet have made and he'll fall right into it, just like I did.

There's a problem here. I've got to think my way

round it. I've got to make sure my secret place stays mine.

My dad, being a soldier, would make an ambush, I suppose. Booby-trap the place like they did in the olden days. Dig a big pit with spikes in the bottom, or have a snare to catch someone by the leg, or use a trip wire that would release a catch and make a rock come smashing down on their head.

I don't know how to do all that and, anyway, what if I hurt someone? The only person I want to hurt is Steve, but if he fell into my trap he'd climb straight out, being so big and strong, and then he'd come right on and kill me. Really kill me.

There's no point in trying to get Steve. The best thing would be for him to go away, right away. Just go away and leave us alone and never come back. Not ever.

Watching the spider gave me the answer. He was mending a hole in his web, and that made me think of the chain link fence. I whizzed back up to the hole, looked carefully up and down the lane and stepped out. Then I stood back and ran my eyes along the whole fence.

A decoy, I thought. That's what I need.

There was another place a bit further on where the fence was broken too. It just needed a bit of work to make a proper hole that you could get through.

It didn't take more than five minutes. I opened up the second place a bit, got inside and trampled around. Not much. I didn't want loads of people to see and get in and start running about all over the railway bank. I made it look so that if Kieran came back he'd think that's what I'd been so interested in.

My plan was even better than I'd thought because there was nothing but thorns and nettles, jungles of them, between this new hole and my secret place. There was no way Kieran or anyone else could get to me if he came through here.

I slipped out again and went back to my hole. No one was around.

I'd got back in through the fence and was trying to camouflage the hole a bit when I heard Kieran coming. I knew it was him. Well, I knew it was a boy, anyway, because he was kicking a can down the lane in front of him. I didn't have time to move further back into my place, so I just froze and shut my eyes.

He was coming nearer and nearer, singing some tuneless song under his breath, dodging and kicking and chasing after his can.

And I was blasting him with thoughtwaves.

Go away, Kieran. I'm not here. No one's here. There's nothing to see, Kieran. Go on, little can. Roll away down the hill. Roll far away, little drinks can.

But it didn't. It rolled just past my hole and stopped, right up against the fence. I opened my eyes a crack and saw the sun glinting off it.

Then I saw Kieran's foot. My heart was pounding so hard I could hear it pumping in my ears, and my eyes were screwed up so tight they hurt. He stood there for about ten years, Kieran did.

What are you doing? I thought, not daring to open my eyes and look in case the movement caught his eye. Go on, Kieran. Please. Go away.

Next I heard the sound of paper tearing and something fluttered to the ground just the other side of the

13

chain link. I did look then. It was a Mars bar wrapper. Kieran was starting on a Mars bar.

My mouth watered so hard I had to swallow, and I thought he'd be sure to hear me, it sounded that loud, but he didn't. He poked out the can from beside the fence with his toe and gave it a kick and off he went, running after it down the lane, only he wasn't singing any more because his mouth was all stuck up with Mars bar.

He hadn't even looked at my decoy hole.

As soon as he'd gone I stood up and bolted for my secret place.

Thank you, God, I said. Thank you.

I sat down on the floor with my back against one of the blocks, and I felt safe.

'We'll get through all right,' I said to the spider. 'You and me. We'll do.'

'We're going to the zoo today,' Steve said. 'A family outing.'

He was in one his loud moods, his I'm-going-to-have-a-good-time-and-you-are-too moods. He's like that when he's with people from work, or down at the pub with her.

'The zoo!' she said, clapping her hands like a little girl.

I didn't dare say I didn't want to go. You don't, with Steve.

He made her put on her stretchy pink top and her tight jeans.

'You won't be able to wear these for much longer,' he said, patting her tummy.

14

She looked quite pleased. I bent down to do up my shoes.

'You can't go in those things. Not on a family outing,' he said, and I froze, ready to put my arm up to protect my head.

He didn't hit me, though. He handed me a shoebox instead.

'New trainers,' he said. 'Thought we'd smarten you up a bit.'

I put the trainers on. They were too small and pinched my toes.

'They'll stretch,' he said. 'Come on, or the place'll be closed before we get there.'

You can have a good time with Steve, once in a while, if nothing goes wrong and you're careful. It was OK at first, our day out at the zoo, in spite of my sore feet.

'Ice creams all round,' he said, as soon as we were in through the gate.

'Oh, I don't know,' she said. 'Ice cream might start me off feeling sick again.'

'Just try one, love,' he said. 'You've got to eat. You've got to keep your strength up.'

He went to the van and came back with three big ones. She took hers and smiled, but she was going pale.

We saw the elephant first. He was standing in a walled-in place, in the open air. There was a big ditch between us and him.

His ears were drooping and he stood with his trunk dangling down, touching the ground, quite still.

'Hey, big fella!' shouted Steve. 'Over here! Look

over here. You a statue, or what? Wave your trunk at Jake, why don't you?'

The elephant wasn't bothered. He moved his ears a bit and whisked something off his rump with the bushy bit on the end of his tail.

'Boring, isn't he?' said Steve. 'They're supposed to be clever, elephants are. You'd think they'd train them to do something. I've paid enough to get us in here.'

'I want to see the monkeys,' she said, clinging on to his arm.

She hadn't eaten her ice cream and melted bits were dribbling down the side.

'Here, watch what you're doing.' He was laughing at her. 'You'll get it all over me. You're not going to eat it, are you? Do you want it, Jake?'

I shook my head.

'You don't want to waste it.' He took it out of her hand and started slurping it up, making gloopy noises. I was starting to feel happy, almost.

Maybe he'll be different now, I thought. Maybe the baby coming has changed him.

'The monkeys are over there.' I ran ahead towards the cages up the hill, going carefully with my toes curled in because the trainers hurt, and then I called back to them over my shoulder, and at that moment I forgot everything bad and I felt free and safe.

There were some little brown monkeys in the first cage, chasing each other, just mucking about really, like a bunch of kids. They were so clever and funny, jumping around, making flying leaps, hanging from one arm and then the other, that you had to laugh. We all did.

'One of them's got a baby, look,' she said, leaning forward to see better. 'Catch me jumping around like that with a baby hanging round my neck.'

'Good thing you're not a monkey, then,' he said, and I saw his hand slide down to her bottom and give it a squeeze.

I moved on round the corner. There was a big monkey here, sitting on a rubber tyre in a corner of a cage. I read the label.

*Chimpanzee*, it said. *Forests of Central Africa.*

There was some dead wood in the cage, a couple of logs set up like branches, and another tyre hanging from a rope like a kind of swing. Bits of fruit and veg were scattered all over the concrete floor.

It's not much like the forests of Central Africa in there, is it? I thought. I bet that's what you're thinking about. I bet you wish you were back there, swinging through the treetops with all your brothers and sisters.

I had a good idea then. My island's been small in my mind, with only room for the tower, and my dad's place, and the apple trees, and the football pitch. But now I want it to be big, a proper island, in the middle of a lake. Or the sea. Yes, the sea, because then there'd be a beach and waves and rock pools and shells. There can't be a drawbridge after all. It's too far away from land. You have to come to it by boat.

And it's going to be a tropical kind of place, big enough to have a bit of forest for chimpanzees and monkeys, and maybe even an elephant or two. And they wouldn't all be stuck in lonely, cruel concrete cages. They'd be free and happy, and they'd go around doing the things they like doing, like eating

17

the silver and golden apples, and messing about in the trees, and playing on the beach.

And they wouldn't be scared of me, because they'd know I'd never, ever hurt them, and they'd look out for me and I'd look out for them and we'd be mates.

Then I heard the two of them coming up behind me.

'Look at him, the big fat slob,' Steve said. 'Let's get him going.'

He bent down and picked up a handful of gravel and threw it at the cage. Most of it bounced off the mesh but some of it got through. I heard it ping on the concrete floor.

'Steve,' she said. 'Don't. You'll hurt him. Someone'll see.'

There were a couple of old people near the cage too. The man had a straw hat on, one with a brim and a black band round it, and the woman's hair was all tight little grey curls. I could tell what they were thinking.

Things were starting to go wrong. I could feel it in the air. A knot was tying itself up in my stomach again, and the hairs on the back of my neck were prickling.

Steve saw them looking at him and his mouth went into a straight line. He leaned over the low fence, right on top of the sign that said, *Warning. These animals are dangerous*, and he began shaking the bars of the cage.

The chimp turned and looked at him. His eyes were big and brown, and they were so sad you could hardly bear to look at them. He put his black hands down on the floor (just like human hands, they were), and stood up and turned his back on us.

'Ha ha! Look at that! Look at his big, bare bum!' shouted Steve. 'Ugly, or what? Not even I'm that ugly, am I, Jake? *Am* I, Jake?'

The chimp bent down over his water bowl, then he turned round and came towards us. He stood up at the bars, and stretched to his full height. I could see him properly then. He was a big guy, a strong proud guy, and I loved him.

He looked down on us as if we were a long, long way away, miles beneath him, then suddenly, before any of us could move, he leaned backwards and lifted his thing and peed. A great spout of wee shot out at Steve. Right at him. Masses of it. It dripped down the front of Steve's shirt and splashed on his shoes.

Steve ducked out the way, then there was a moment of silence that lasted about a week, and Steve roared, and she stepped back with her hand over her mouth, and the man in the hat said, in a posh voice, 'Serves him right, the lout,' and the woman with the grey curls said, 'As you say, dear,' and then they walked away.

But I hardly noticed them because I'd started to giggle, and once I started I couldn't stop, and then I was laughing so hard I was choking on it, gasping and staggering about, and I could feel tears of laughter spurting out of my eyes, and I knew my face had gone scarlet.

I stopped laughing, though, stopped dead, when he caught hold of my arm. His fingers were like steel nails. He jerked me towards him till his face was

19

inches from mine. His eyes were splinters of glass and his mouth was an iron trap.

'Laughing, are you? Think it's funny, do you? I'll show you. I'll teach you what's funny, so you won't ever forget again.'

If I turn my head, even a little bit, I can feel shoots of pain like flames, running through it and down into my shoulders, and my mouth's numb and swollen up and it hurts all over me, everywhere.

He didn't start till we got home. He never does it in front of other people. This time he didn't bother to keep off my face. He went for everything. Every bit of me, punching and kicking and shaking.

'Don't, Steve,' I kept crying. 'Stop it. Please. Don't.'

The worse thing was that I wet myself. I couldn't help it. And then I felt worthless and small, lost and worthless, as if there was nothing left inside me. It was all beaten out.

I've got to go. I can't stay here with them any more. I've got to get away before he kills me.

I've put a few things in my bag – a sweater, and my raincoat, some socks and my fluffy duck. I'll be all right in my secret place, as long as this nice weather lasts. I've got a bit of money. It's not much, but it'll do for a few days, while I think things out. Make a plan. Decide what I'm going to do.

I got out of the house all right without her hearing me. Steve had gone down the pub anyway, and she was banging things round in the kitchen.

I felt bad about leaving her. She needs someone to

protect her. I've never been able to do that, but I've been useful, in a way. When Steve was going to thump someone he'd go for me first, and sometimes he'd stop there.

But maybe it's all my fault anyway. Maybe it's me that makes him violent. If I'm not there maybe she'll be all right.

Anyway, what use is anyone to anyone when all they can do is pee in their pants?

I went down the lane towards my secret place, but I knew even before I got to the hole in the fence that something was wrong. The hole had been wrenched wide open and all my camouflage stuff had been chucked about.

People had been in my secret place. Someone had sprayed *Kieran's a wanker* on one of the concrete blocks in white paint, and there were a whole bunch of tags.

I didn't know the tags. They weren't anyone's I knew.

The spider's web had gone. That was the worst thing. There were just a few silky strands blowing in the breeze. I couldn't see the spider anywhere, though I looked round as much as I could.

I don't blame you, I said silently to the spider. What's the point of sticking around here? What's the point of waiting for me? There's nothing left inside me.

In my dream house there'll be a special place for webs, I started to tell him, but then I stopped. I didn't want to think about my dream house. I was afraid that if I did the tower would come crashing down with me inside it and everything around it would be destroyed.

There wasn't any point in staying in my secret place because it wasn't mine any more. And now I didn't have anywhere to go. Nowhere. I'd have to go back to them. There was no point in running away.

But then, in the sunshine, I saw the flash of light on a line of shiny metal. Down there in front of me was the railway line.

I went down to the railway line and I thought, The next train that comes along, I'm going to do it. I'm going to jump in front of it.

It was partly because of the baby, see? I thought I could go on if it was just myself, go on ducking and diving and keeping out of his way, pretending I don't see when he mashes her up just like she doesn't look when it's me, but I wouldn't be able to do that any more when the baby was there. I couldn't turn a blind eye then. I'd have to stay around and look out for it all the time, only I wouldn't be brave enough. All I'd do is stand there and cry and pee in my pants.

I looked down at the rails, all light and shiny where the wheels go over them, and it was as if they were calling to me, telling me to lie down on them.

I'll do it now, I thought. The next one that comes.

It came sooner than I'd expected. I hadn't had time to settle my mind. I heard the rails hum first and then sing and rattle, the way they do, and I thought, OK. OK. Let's wait a bit. Let it come nearer.

But it came so suddenly, with a whoosh and a roar and a blast of wind in my face that I was taken by surprise. I stepped back. I had to.

The next one, I thought.

I was looking down at the wheels. They were rushing along in a blur of speed. I thought, If I could just see the shape of one it would be good, to know what I'm in for, but I couldn't make one out. Not at that speed. The wheels had disappeared and all that was left were screaming, throbbing lines of metal, not real at all.

I didn't look up at the windows till the train was nearly past. But I did then, and I saw her.

A little child was standing up with her hands pressed against the window. She had a tangle of dark hair round her face. A little, thin face it was. Her mouth was open as if she was calling out to me, and I could see her eyes, wide and frightened. She seemed to be begging me for something. A second later she'd gone.

I swear to God it was the baby. My sister. She was up there, looking down at me, and she was calling out, 'Stay, Jake. Don't go. I need you.'

I got away from the railway line and stumbled over this old tyre that someone must have chucked down here. My knees are so weak I couldn't stand up if I tried, and my heart's banging away like a demented drum kit. There's this whistling noise in my ears, and my head's pounding, and all I can think is, I nearly did it. I nearly topped myself. I must have been crazy.

The sun's setting now, but it's still bright, a spring sun, the sort that comes on strong when you're out of the wind, and it's warming up my hands and face. I can feel it through my trouser legs and on the sore places on my face.

It feels good. I'm starting to hear things again: the bird on the top of the tree, and the traffic from the main road, and some kids shouting on the far side of the track.

Everything's suddenly so beautiful that I want to put my head down on my knees and cry.

Kieran made me jump. I didn't hear him coming. I was still crying a bit, feeling shaky and weird and out of it, when he said, 'Hello'.

He'd slid down the bit of bank behind me and landed up right next to me.

'You're Jake, aren't you?' he said.

I think I said, 'Go away and leave me alone,' but I'm not sure. Anyway he didn't hear it, whatever I said, partly because my voice was still funny with crying, but mostly because he was staring at me so hard.

'Wow,' he said. 'What happened to your face?'

I wasn't ready for this, for making up excuses, and thinking my way out of it, and finding somewhere to sneak off to, like I usually do. There was nowhere to go here, and anyway, Kieran wasn't going to let me.

'Fell off my bike,' I said.

'Under a bus, or what? Bet they had to tow the bus away. You look amazing. Like something on telly. Does it hurt?'

'A bit.'

I shifted along the bank away from him. I tried to stand up, but my legs were too weak. They'd begun to stiffen up with all the bruises on them. I didn't mean to, but I made a sort of groaning noise, and then I stopped trying to move.

'Did you go to the hospital?' said Kieran. 'You ought to. You could have gangrene or something.'

'It's OK. The doctor says I'm fine.'

In my head I was saying, Go away. Just get up and go away.

'I bet the bike was a wreck.'

I nodded, then wished I hadn't. Shooting pains like needles shot up my neck through my head.

'Was it a new one? What sort was it?'

'I dunno. It wasn't mine. I borrowed it. I don't want to talk about it any more.'

'Oh, OK.' He took that. 'It's the shock, isn't it? Did they give you tea with masses of sugar in it? That's what you do with shock.'

I didn't say anything. I couldn't. My head was spinning like I was going to pass out.

'You've gone a funny colour,' said Kieran. 'Yellow. Or green even.'

I put my head down between my knees again. The aching was worse like that but the spinning stopped.

'I'm going to get my nan,' said Kieran. 'She used to work at the hospital. You ought to see someone. She'll know what to do.'

He stood up. The shock sent the faintness away.

'No!' I said, lifting up my head, though for a moment I'd wanted to say, Yes, get her. Take me there. Help me.

Instead I said, 'Don't bother. I'm all right. Really.'

He stood there looking down at me, then he said, 'OK,' but he didn't sound as if he meant it.

I had to think of something to stop him going.

'Who did all those tags and stuff up there?' I said.

He burst out laughing. He looked nice when he laughed. He's got this yellow curly hair and it shook about, and his eyes were screwed up, and his mouth (it's a big one) was wide open, and he crashed back down on to the bank beside me. He was laughing properly, right up from his stomach, not giggling or sniggering or anything. It was a riotous sort of noise. It warmed me up a bit. Took some of the ache away.

'That was Marty and his lot,' he said at last. 'They were down by the bridge. They'd climbed over the wall and were graffing up the back of it. Thought they were being hard. So I called out, "Rubbish tags" and stuff like that, just to wind them up, and they all came after me. You should have seen them! Luke fell over his big feet, and David's can was leaking and he got purple paint all down his front, and old Simon was puffing along at the back shouting, "Wait for me!" I could hardly run for laughing.'

'You came in here with them after you,' I said.

'Yes. I got through the hole in the fence . . .'

'How did you know about the hole?'

'I saw you looking at it the other day, didn't I? You hid it OK, but I found it again. I came in on my own after you'd gone. Had a look around. It's quiet here. I like it.'

He was looking at me again, but I didn't say anything.

'Anyway, they saw me come in through the hole and came straight in after me. Bang, crash. I hid up by the fence in those bushes, and they shouted around for a bit and sprayed that stuff and then they went off, I don't know where.'

'Not coming back, are they? Do you know?'

He could tell I was worried about it.

'No,' he said, and I noticed something about Kieran then. He's good at picking up what other people are thinking. He understands things.

He was starting to laugh again.

'One of them, the dozy one, Neville, he got into the nettles up there, by the fence. He was stung to bits, going, "Wah! Get me out of here!" And Marty got all tangled up in the thorny stuff. You should have heard them cussing! I had to stuff my hands into my mouth to stop laughing out loud. Anyway, you don't need to worry about Marty. He's all mouth. Not scared of him really, are you?'

I didn't dare shake my head again.

'No,' I said. 'I'm not scared of Marty. I don't want him coming here, that's all.'

Kieran was looking round again, as if he was weighing the place up.

'I know what you mean. It's nice here. It's your place though, isn't it? You found it.'

I knew what he wanted me to say and I said it, I don't know why.

'Yes, but you can come back again if you like. I don't mind. I'd quite like it, really.'

We didn't notice that the sun had gone in till we both felt cold, and looked up, and saw a big black cloud had come over.

Kieran said, 'I'm off before it rains.'

He stood up, and I did too. I felt wobbly again when I was on my feet but I managed all right. I just

27

stood for a minute, until I felt stronger, then we went up the bank together.

'There was a spider in here the other day,' Kieran said, as we walked between the blocks, right through what had been my secret place. 'I didn't use to like spiders but he was all right. He made a brilliant web.'

'Marty's lot broke it,' I said.

'Tossers,' said Kieran.

We went through the hole in the fence and walked up the lane together. I wanted to go slowly, partly because I was sore all over, and partly because I didn't want to get there, but Kieran kept going faster because he didn't want to get wet.

I don't have to go straight in, I thought. I'll wait around outside for a bit. Get the timing right.

There's a T-junction at the top of the lane where the road goes past. Kieran's house was off to the left, over the railway bridge, but to get to our flats you have to go right.

We hadn't quite got up to the T-junction when I got a fright. Steve was walking along the road ahead. The first drops of rain were falling and the wind was cold. He'd turned up his collar and had his head down and his fists were in his pockets.

I made a sort of mewing noise, I know I did, before I could stop myself, and ducked sideways behind a tree.

'What's got into you?' Kieran said, quite loudly.

'Shut up, shut up,' I said, and I leaned my forehead against the tree trunk and shut my eyes and felt a tremble go right through me, all the way down, from my ears to my toes.

'Is it that man?' Kieran said, more quietly. 'Why are you scared? Is he your dad, or what?'

'My stepdad.'

'Was it his bike? The one you wrecked?'

I couldn't say anything. I just looked at him, and then the rain came down all of a sudden, in a great whoosh, and Kieran yelled, 'I'm off. See you,' and started tearing down the road towards the bridge, and I looked back to see if Steve had gone, and he had. So I turned right, and hobbled home with my knees weak with fright because I didn't know what I'd find when I got there.

When I got to the entrance of our little block of flats, I suddenly wanted to hurry. I got myself up the stairs and rattled the letter box.

She opened the door at once. She'd been crying and her face was red, but he hadn't hit her. At least, I didn't think so.

'Oh, Jake,' she said. 'Jakey. I was sure he'd killed you. I thought you'd gone off and I'd never see you again.'

'I nearly did,' I said. 'I was going to.'

She hugged me. It hurt my sore places, and she noticed me pulling back so she let go. I wished I hadn't flinched. I liked the feelings of her arms round me.

'I'm sorry. Oh, Jake, I'm so sorry,' she said. 'It's never going to happen again. I promise you, Jakey, on my life.'

She'd promised like that before, so I didn't think much of it. I didn't say anything. I just went on standing there, remembering the feeling of her holding me. She came closer again and put her arm gently round my shoulders. There were tears sliding down my cheeks. I didn't even realize till the salt stung the place where my lip had split. I let them go on falling. I didn't want to move in case she took her arm away.

'Mum,' I whispered to myself. 'Mum.'

She dropped her arm after a bit and looked at me, really looked, turning my head with one finger to see all the damage he'd done.

'Do you need the hospital?' she said. 'Do you want me to take you up there?'

'No. What's the point? There's nothing broken.'

She took my hand and led me like a baby into her bedroom.

'Sit down,' she said, 'while I finish packing.'

She had a suitcase open on the bed and was putting stuff into it. Her things were falling out of drawers all over the floor and in a mess on the bed. My heart nearly stopped beating with the shock.

'Packing? What do you mean? You're not leaving, are you? Where are you going?'

'Not me. Us. You and me. We're getting out.' She was cramming her make-up into a little bag. 'We're going, Jake. I'm leaving him and you're coming with me. Now. Before he gets back from the pub.'

My heart started again with a violent kick. There was a kind of explosion in my head. It was either a beautiful firework, or a scary bomb, I couldn't tell which.

'Where to, Mum? Where are we going?'

She didn't answer. She piled more stuff into her suitcase and leaned on it to close it.

'I'll tell you on the way. Get your stuff and let's get out. He might be back any minute.'

She pulled another suitcase out from under the bed.

'Here. Put your things in that.'

I was off the bed in a flash, and hobbling to my bedroom. I'd dropped my little rucksack by the front door and I picked it up and took it to my room. I stuffed it straight into the case then looked round.

Earlier, when I'd packed the rucksack, I'd known in my heart that I was coming back. This was different. This was her and me together. Mum and me. It was real.

It didn't take long to fill the suitcase. There wasn't much I wanted to take with me out of that flat.

She was standing at the door of my bedroom with her coat on as I zipped the suitcase up.

'You ready? Come on.'

We went out through the front door and she shut it with a bang. She was off down the stairs before the sound had died away, bumping her heavy suitcase down the steps.

We stopped for a moment at the entrance to the building. It was nearly dark by now and the rain was pelting down.

'Tough,' she said, turning up her collar. 'Bit of rain won't hurt us. Come on, Jake.'

'Where are we going?' I limped after her, trying to ignore the rain that was streaming down my face. 'Not the women's refuge, is it?'

We'd never been to it, but she'd often told Steve she'd go there, anytime he turned nasty. She'd used it

31

as a threat. I didn't like the sound of the refuge. I didn't even know where it was.

'No,' she said. The weight of her suitcase was pulling her right over and her knees were buckling. She didn't say any more till we got to the bus shelter. It was lucky, because no one else was in it. No one else had been mad enough to go out in all that rain.

'Why not the refuge, Mum?'

'Because they'll take one look at you and get on to the Social and you'll end up in care, that's why not. I'm not letting that happen to you, Jake. Not ever.'

'Where are we going, then?'

She was hunting in her purse for the change for when the bus came along, and she didn't look at me.

'We're not sleeping rough, are we?' I said. 'Not in this rain?'

The thought of it, being out in the cold and wet all night made me shiver all over and a dreadful desolate feeling swept over me. Earlier, I'd imagined myself dossing down in my secret place, but it had been daylight then, and the sun had been shining, and it had been dry.

She sat down on the bench and looked up the road, watching anxiously for the bus's headlights. Steve would come past here on his way home, and we'd be caught like rats if the bus didn't come soon.

'We're going to Mrs Judd,' she said.

Her voice sounded thin, as if her throat was tight. She was dead nervous, I could tell.

Then it hit me.

Judd. That was my dad's name. Danny Judd.

'You mean we're going to find my dad?'

'No.' She shook her head violently. 'His mum. She

never did anything for you. Not that I ever asked. I never wanted to see the old cow, not after she turned Danny against me. But she owes us, Jake. She's your grandma. She's got to take us in. She has to.'

But you don't think she will, I thought.

I screwed up my eyes and took a deep breath, trying to steady myself. Things were happening too fast. I felt I was in a dream, or rather, a nightmare.

I can't help it, but here on the bus (we're sitting on the long seats that face inwards in case we pass Steve and he sees us), I've gone off into a daydream.

I'm imagining Mrs Judd, my grandma, and her house.

I can see it in my head. It's like on a greeting card, with yellow stone walls, and a front door in the middle. There's a big window on either side, and a garden in front with lots of flowers, and an old tree with a swing hanging from it.

My grandma sees us plodding up the path and she flings the door open, and says, 'This must be Jake. Why didn't you come before, Marie? We've been waiting for you all these years.'

And someone else comes out from behind her, a soldier, in a beautiful scarlet uniform with medals on his chest and stripes on his arm, and he salutes me, and says, 'Welcome home, son.'

'We're here, this is it, I think,' Mum said, rubbing the condensation off the glass to peer out of the bus's window, and we dragged our suitcases from the luggage place and stepped off the bus into the dark and the rain.

My daydream vanished like a puff of steam blowing away in the wind.

'Don't let's go there, Mum,' I said, catching at her sleeve. 'Let's try the refuge. I'll tell them I was in a fight with some kids. I won't let the Social take me away.'

It wasn't very far from the bus stop to Mrs Judd's house. Just as well, really, because I was hanging back all the way, and if it had been much further I'd have turned round and run away. And she'd have come on behind me. She was more scared than I was, I could tell.

The house wasn't a bit like the one I'd imagined. Well, I knew it wouldn't be. It was in a terrace, set back a bit from the road, with a bit of garden in the front. There weren't any roses that I could see, but there were some things growing there, looking nicely kept, and a little clipped hedge, and a dustbin just by the gate with the lid clamped on.

There was someone in the front room. You could see the chink of light coming through the gap in the curtains, and the TV was on.

Mum put her suitcase down and looked up at the place. Her hair was sopping wet, straggling down over her face, and her mascara was running. She looked cold and shivery. And I must have looked like something out of a war film, all beaten up and soaked to the skin.

'It's no good. We can't. Please, Mum, let's go,' I said.

It wasn't Mrs Judd that really scared me, even though I thought she might turn nasty. The thing that was doing my head in and turning my stomach over was the thought that he might open the door. My dad. And he might look at me scornfully, or not look at me properly at all, and say, 'Bugger off. Stay out of my life, you little toad. I don't ever want to see you again.'

I turned round, ready to bolt for the gate. She dropped her suitcase on the doorstep, ran back, grabbed me by the arm and yanked me up the little path to the door again.

'If you want to sleep out in the rain, go ahead. I don't,' she said, and pressed the bell.

As soon as she'd done it she looked terrified, and she pulled me up close to her.

A shadow loomed up behind the bubbly glass of the little panes in the top half of the door, and it opened.

Mrs Judd, my grandma, stood there.

She was a big woman. Heavy. She was wearing black trousers and an orange jumper, and from where we were standing, two steps below her, she looked massive. I couldn't see her face because the light was behind her head, but I could tell by the way she was standing that she wasn't impressed by what had fetched up on her front steps.

'Can't you read the sign?' she said, stabbing her finger at a little blue sticker on the doorpost. 'We do not buy or sell at the door.'

'We haven't come to buy or sell anything, Mrs Judd,' my mum said. She sounded uptight and angry, like she does when she's nervous.

Mrs Judd leaned forward to take a closer look when she heard her own name.

'It's me, Marie,' Mum said. 'Don't you remember me?'

Mrs Judd started back, then she gave a little laugh, half angry, half mocking.

'Marie Lindsay. Well, I never. Fancy you turning up like a bad penny after all these years. I suppose you're after Danny again. You've come to the wrong place. He's not here, and even if he is, he wouldn't give you the time of day.'

Mum had let go of me. She was standing with her two feet planted square in front of the door and her arms were crossed on her chest.

'Don't I know it,' she said. 'I wouldn't expect anything better from him.'

'Just as well, then,' said Mrs Judd.

'Seeing as how,' Mum went on, 'he turned his back and walked away from his own baby.'

Mrs Judd snorted.

'But you're Jake's grandma,' Mum said, less certainly now, 'and I thought at least you . . . that you might . . .'

Her voice trailed away and her arms dropped to her side. Mrs Judd turned her head towards me for the first time. I tried to smile a bit and look nice. First impressions are important, I know that much. I forgot for a moment that my face looked as if a bulldozer had pushed it in. Anyway, it didn't impress Mrs Judd.

'Come off it, Marie,' she said, stepping backwards as if she was about to shut the door. 'You tried that on years ago. You're not getting one over on me now.'

A kind of wail came out of Mum's throat.

'You old bitch! You and your son! Got me up the spout and left me on my own. Not a penny to help out.' She was crying now, and her voice was coming out trembly. 'Not so much as a Christmas card for the kid. How do you expect me to manage? Where do you want us to go? A decent person wouldn't turn a dog out on a night like this, never mind their own flesh and blood.' She bent to pick up her suitcase. 'Come on, Jake.'

'The police station's down at the end of the road. Turn left, then right,' Mrs Judd said. 'They'll sort you out. Or are you too scared to show yourself? It was you, wasn't it, who did that to the kid's face? You beat him up, didn't you?'

I'd been just standing there all this time, not saying anything, but that did it.

'She never touched me,' I shouted. 'Never. It was Steve. That's why we ran away. And you can tell my dad, next time you see him that I . . .'

Things were building up inside me, things I wanted to say. This might be my only chance, ever, of getting a message through to him. The trouble was, I couldn't find the words. And I'd started crying, like a silly kid.

'You can tell him,' I said, swallowing all the time, 'that I don't blame him. I never have. I don't want to cause him any trouble. I've still got the fluffy duck he gave me when he came to see me in the hospital. I never let Steve get hold of it. Not once.'

Mrs Judd's hand dropped away from the door and she took a step forward, but then she felt the rain on her hair and moved back under cover again.

'You shouldn't have done that, Marie,' she said.

'You shouldn't have told the boy lies. Danny's not his father. You know it. I know it. That was wrong.'

I wanted to spit at her.

'He is! He is my dad!' I yelled at her. 'Mum's never lied to me. Why should she? Anyway, he wouldn't have come to see me in the hospital, would he? He wouldn't have written that letter, would he?'

Mrs Judd looked puzzled for a moment, then she shook her head pityingly.

'What about your family, Marie?' she said, her voice a little bit softer. 'I'm sure they'd help you out if you're stuck for place to go.'

Mum made an angry noise but didn't answer.

'You should have gone to your own mother, not me,' Mrs Judd said. 'Where is she anyway?'

'How should I know?' Mum snapped out. 'Ask the children's home where she dumped me. I never bothered.'

Neither of them did anything for a moment, then Mum said, 'It's you or the refuge. If I take him there in this state, the Social will get him. They'll put him in Willowbank like they did with me.'

Mrs Judd seemed to dither all of a sudden. She was looking at me, but I didn't look back. What was the point?

Mum waited a moment, then she said, 'OK, I get it. I didn't expect anything better from you anyway. Come on, Jake. We're not wanted here.'

She'd gone sort of saggy in the middle, and when she bent down to pick up her suitcase she could hardly lift it off the ground.

'Leave it. I'll take it for a bit,' I said.

We got to the gate, and I said, 'Which way? Right

or left?' and she started laughing. It was scarier than shouting or carrying on. Scarier even than crying. She just kept laughing and saying, 'I don't know and I don't care. What's the difference? Right or left, Jake. Whichever you like. It's all the same to me.'

A dreadful cold, despairing feeling was closing in on me. I looked back to the house. Mrs Judd was still standing at the open door, her hands clasped together.

'Marie,' she called out. 'I'll give you some money for a taxi. Come back here. You can't take the kid wandering round the streets in this weather. He'll catch his death.'

'Stuff your money, you old bag,' shouted Mum. 'I wouldn't touch it if you begged me.'

The thought of climbing into a warm dry taxi was too much for me.

'Mum,' I said. 'Please. I'm freezing.'

'Jake! It's Jake, isn't it?' Mrs Judd said. 'Come back here. I'm not going to bite you. Come on. Look, I'll give you a tenner. Get yourself and your mum into the warm somewhere, OK?'

I went back up to the door. She stepped inside and turned her back on me to open her handbag which was on a little table in the hall. For the first time I saw a picture hanging on the wall behind her. As I looked up at it, the hood of my jacket fell back off my head.

'Mrs Judd,' I said, 'why have you got a picture of me on your wall?'
She stiffened, and shut the clip on her handbag with a loud snapping noise.

'Try anything, wouldn't you?' she said. 'That's not you. That's Danny, as you well know.'
Then she turned back to me with a couple of fivers in her hand.

'Jake!' Mum was shouting from the gate. 'Come here. Don't touch her money. Get away from her.'

I don't suppose Mrs Judd had seen me properly till then. I'd had my hood up and, like I keep saying, my face wasn't exactly recognizable. Anyway, that was the moment when it happened. I think what did it was seeing the way my hair shoots straight up from my forehead, just like the boy in the photo. Whatever it was, something clicked in her eyes. Click. Like that. She recognized me.

She put a hand up to the side of her face.

'My God,' she said. 'It is. Danny.'

Mum and I were sitting on the edge of the sofa in Mrs Judd's front room. We'd taken our outdoor things off and dumped them in the hall, but my other clothes underneath were wet and I was shivering. I could hear Mrs Judd in her kitchen at the back, making tea.

Mum's back was straight and her cheeks were red and she was saying things under her breath, nodding her head. It looked like she was working herself up, getting ready all the things she wanted to say to Mrs Judd. I'd never seen her like this before. I'd never known her to fight back.

She'll get us thrown out if she loses her rag, I told myself, and all I could think of was being outside in the cold and the wet, and wanting to stay in here and get warm.

'Do I really look like him?' I said, touching her arm. 'Like my dad? You never said.'

I wanted to take her mind off being angry, but it didn't work. She didn't notice I'd said anything.

I gave up and looked round the room. It was nice. Very clean and tidy, anyway. The little blue cushions on the sofa (four of them) were balanced upright on their corners, and there were lace mats under all the vases and jugs and china statues she'd arranged on a sort of sideboard thing.

The only way you could tell someone lived here was the dent in the seat of an older chair with wooden arms pulled up near the gas fire, and a pair of glasses on the table next to it.

Mrs Judd came back in carrying a tray. Her hands were shaking and the mugs were rattling against each other.

'Pull that other chair up to the fire,' she said, looking at me, not at Mum. 'You look half frozen.'

I didn't move. She put the tray down on the little table, bent over to turn the gas up and straightened up again.

'Sugar, Marie?'

'No,' said Mum, stretching out her hand for the mug.

'What about you, Jake?'

She was staring at me as if I was a ghost.

'Two please, Mrs Judd,' I said.

I remembered what Kieran had said about sweet tea being good for shock. That's what his nan gave him when he got beaten up, probably, and now here I was with my own nan offering some to me. Weird.

She gave me the tea and sat down in her chair again.

'I don't know what to say,' she said. 'It's a shock, just seeing him like that. He's Danny all over again. It seems I did you an injustice, Marie. If I'd thought, for one moment . . .'

Mum gave an angry laugh.

'Oh, you thought all right. You thought I was a lying, cheating little money-grabber, trying to get my hooks into your precious Danny. You thought I was the scum of the earth.'

The warmth of the tea, all hot and sugary, began to spread through me as I sipped it. I held the mug on my knees with my hands cupped round it. The heat was running up my arms and down my legs, but inside I was beginning to shrivel up again at the angry sound in Mum's voice.

Mrs Judd put her mug down on the tray. Her back had stiffened now.

'If you mean did I want Danny going off and getting led into all kinds of things, no, I didn't.'

'Led into? *Led into*?' Mum's voice was rising. 'Got no idea, have you? They were trouble, the pair of them, Danny Judd and Steve Barlow. Up for anything. It was them did the leading.'

I felt as if an electric shock had run through me, a horrible tingling feeling.

'What? Steve and my dad? You mean they were mates? You never said that, Mum. I never knew that.'

'You can't pull that one on me.' Mrs Judd's face was going red. 'I kept Danny away from Steve

Barlow. He was a bad influence. In trouble from the time he could walk. I never allowed him—'

Mum snorted.

'You don't know the half of it. Danny was out of his bedroom window and down the drainpipe every other night. Good training, he said, for when he was in the SAS. They were after me night after night, the two of them. Wouldn't leave me in peace.'

Mrs Judd pounced on this like a dog on a titbit.

'So how was anyone to know, when you got pregnant, who the father was? I used to see you, down by the cinema, all dolled up in your skimpy little skirts, shrieking and falling about with half the boys in town.'

Mum quivered.

'I never looked at anyone but Danny. Never went with anyone. He was the only one. I thought I was going to die when he ran off and left me.'

Mrs Judd was like someone left behind in a race, trying to catch up. I felt the same, about a mile back and out of breath.

'That drainpipe, it wouldn't have held his weight,' she said. 'It kept coming loose. Jake kept having to fix it.'

'I can't have done,' I said. 'I wasn't even here.'

'Not you. Danny's dad.'

'You mean my grandad?' I hadn't bargained for a grandad.

She looked surprised.

'Yes, I suppose so. Yes, of course. Your grandfather. Are you sure you don't want to sit nearer the fire, dear? Have some more tea.'

'But he's got the same name as me,' I said.

Mum looked down at me, and I had the feeling she'd forgotten for a while that I was there.

'Danny chose your name. We agreed on it before you were born. Jake for a boy. Rosalie Michelle for a girl. I'd got used to it. I liked it. So I kept to it even after he ditched me.'

'He always loved his dad,' Mrs Judd said, looking away from me into the fire. 'He never got over him dying like that.'

'He's dead, then, my grandad?' I said.

'Yes,' said Mrs Judd. 'When Danny was fourteen. You've got to remember that, Marie. He was only sixteen when he – when you had the baby.'

The steam had started going out of Mum but when Mrs Judd said that it fizzed right up again.

'Sixteen! Big deal! I was sixteen too. Sixteen, on my own, and pregnant.'

Mrs Judd was picking at the bottom of her orange sweater.

'Why didn't he come and tell me? If he'd only owned up to it—'

'Tell you?' The scorn in Mum's voice could have withered the plants on the windowsill. 'I can see it, can't you? "Oh, Mummy, all those nights you thought I was up in bed reading my comics and cuddling my teddy bear, I was down behind the Odeon smashing up the call boxes and having it off with Marie." Scared stiff, he was, your precious Danny. Fight it out with anyone, down in town, but when it came to him facing up to his own mum, when it came to standing by his girlfriend and looking after his own kid, he was pathetic. A loser.'

Mrs Judd seemed about to say something angry.

Her eyes were locked on to Mum's, and they were staring at each other. There was a question I'd been dying to ask, and at last I got it out.

'Where is he, my dad? Am I going to see him?'

'He's in Lancashire,' said Mrs Judd, her eyes still on Mum, 'and when he gets back he's going to get one hell of a shock. I never thought – I never dreamed – I can't believe it, Marie. I can't get over it.'

'But, Mrs Judd,' I said, 'look on the bright side. If it hadn't happened, I wouldn't be here, would I?'

For some reason, that made her laugh, and even Mum's face cracked into half a smile. She stood up, pulled the other chair over to the fire and put her hands out to the warmth.

'Look,' she said. 'I didn't come here to ask for charity. I'm in a hole, that's all, and I need a bit of help. Which, I think you'll agree, I've got a right to.'

She stuck her chin out as though she expected Mrs Judd to argue, but Mrs Judd just nodded.

'It's for Jake, see?' Mum went on, as if talking had become more difficult. 'I wouldn't have come on my own account.'

'Jake said something about Steve,' said Mrs Judd, leaning forward too. 'Not Steve Barlow, surely? You're not shacked up with him, are you, Marie?'

Mum pulled back.

'I've been married – well, as good as – to Steve ever since Jake was a baby. You can turn your nose up, but he was the only one who stuck around. I kept him off as long as I could. Thought Danny might come back, didn't I? But he didn't, so I gave in in the end. You can say what you like about Steve, but he's loyal, which is more than you can say for some. And he gave us a home.'

She stopped and pushed her hair back from her face. It had been drying off and was going frizzy round the edges.

'The thing is,' she went on, 'he keeps going after Jake. It was OK when Jake was little, well, most of the time. I used to keep Jake out of his way. It was me he went for then, being so jealous as he is. Locked me in, sometimes, he was that crazy. Broke my rib once. Now it's Jake he goes for. It seems the more Jake turns out looking like Danny, the more it riles him.'

I realized my mouth had fallen open. Things were dropping into place like coins into slots. Steve didn't hate me because I was me, but because I looked like my dad. That was OK by me. That was just fine by me.

The thing in the back of my mind, though, the thing that was bothering me now was that bit about Steve and my dad being mates. If my dad liked Steve that much, maybe he was the same kind of person. Maybe he wasn't like I'd always imagined him, and he was a puncher and a beater too.

Perhaps it was that thought, or maybe it was not having eaten anything since the ice cream at the zoo, centuries ago, or the knocks to my head, or getting so cold and wet. Anyway, the room and Mum and Mrs Judd and the china ornaments and the gas fire began to go round and round, and I started to fall. I didn't even feel myself landing on the floor.

*

'Take his legs. Get him back up on the cushions.'

Mrs Judd's voice came from a long way away.

'Jake! Can you hear me? Open your eyes, love. Please!'

It was Mum, and she sounded upset.

I felt them lift me and guessed I was lying on the sofa. It was soft anyway, and smelt of old cloth. I didn't dare open my eyes in case I passed out again.

'He's not got concussion, has he?' Mrs Judd sounded disapproving. 'You shouldn't have let him out, Marie, after a head injury. He should have gone to bed and stayed there.'

'Oh?' Mum flared up. 'That's what I should have done, is it? Put him in his bed and wait for Steve to come back and finish him off after he'd tanked himself up at the pub? That's all you know about it.' Her voice softened. 'Jake, love, please. Can you hear me, darling? Open your eyes.'

It took more effort than pushing a bus up Mount Everest, but I got my lids open, and gave her a bit of a smile. Then I let them close again.

'There. He's coming round,' said Mum. 'You'll be all right in a minute, Jake. Just lie still.'

'I ought to get the doctor,' said Mrs Judd.

'He didn't have his tea,' said Mum, 'or anything at midday either, come to think of it.'

'Why didn't you say?' Mrs Judd sounded almost relieved. 'Danny always used to come over funny if he missed a meal. I'll do some beans on toast. You could probably do with some and all.'

I heard the door open and close.

Mum was kneeling on the floor beside the sofa. I could feel her presence really close to me, and smell the peachy stuff she put on her face. She was holding my hand in one of hers and stroking it with the other. It felt great.

'Mum,' I managed to croak out.

'Oh, Jake,' she said, all choked up. 'You looked so bad I was scared. I thought the old bat would go for the police and have you taken away. Can you sit up a bit? She's getting you something to eat.'

'I'm not hungry,' I whispered. 'Just really, really tired. Can we stay here? I don't want to go out again.'

'You're not going to,' Mum said, in her new fighting voice. 'You're going to sleep here tonight. Me too.'

She took her hands away. I wanted to grab hold and keep her there, but I didn't.

'I'll be back in a minute,' she said, and went out of the room.

When she opened the door I caught a whiff of the baked beans, and the smell turned me up. I rolled over to face the back of the sofa and closed my eyes again. I could feel sleep creep up through me like a thick fog.

A bit later, I heard them come back into the room, and Mum said, 'It's no good. He's dead asleep. You can never wake him up once he's gone right off.'

And Mrs Judd said, 'We'd better leave him here, then. I'll get a blanket down. You can sleep in the back room tonight, Marie.'

There was a bit of coming and going, and then a couple of blankets were tucked round me, and someone turned off the fire and switched out the lights, and the fog rolled on over me and swallowed me right up.

*

I feel as if I was in church. This room is sort of holy, and I don't dare touch a single thing. Only look. It's OK to look.

It's his room. I'm lying in his bed.

The thought does my head in, it's so unreal.

You can tell he left home when he was young, only a couple of years older than me, because there are boys' things still in here. There's a model of a B52 bomber on the shelf above his bed, and a biker poster stuck up behind the door.

There's other stuff too, though. Army stuff. A picture of a badge in a frame, and a shield like you get if you've won a race.

The best thing is a photo of a whole lot of soldiers in their combat gear, in a desert somewhere, perched all over a tank. They're grinning and waving and giving the V sign. I've looked and looked at it, till my eyes have gone crossed, trying to work out which one's him.

That's so pathetic. I can't even tell which man is my own dad.

My best guess is the guy at the back, with his face a bit in the shade.

There's another photo too, much posher, with a lot more soldiers in really smart uniforms. They're standing in rows with the real toffs sitting in chairs in front. The trouble is, they're all wearing caps with the brims down over their noses, so I can't see which one has the tufty hair. None of them are smiling. The sergeant major's just yelled at them, 'Eyes front! Stand to attention! Wipe that smile off your face, you horrible little man!'

There are three bedrooms in this house. Mrs

Judd's is at the front, and there's another quite big one at the back, next to the bathroom. And this little one, my dad's old room, is over the front door.

Why didn't they give him the bigger room at the back? They didn't have any other kids. They didn't have to stick him in here.

This room is so small he probably used to lie here on the bed, like I'm doing now, and reach out to take something off the table by the far wall, just by stretching his arm out. And if he'd had the cupboard door open, he could have chucked things straight into it without getting up. That's what I'd do anyway, if this was my room.

Maybe he chose this room, though. Maybe he's like me, and he likes small spaces where you can feel safe, places like the room up the tower in my dream house, or my secret place by the railway line, before the taggers got to it.

When he was little, he probably used to get in here and shut the door and sit with his back against it. And he screwed up his eyes and didn't breathe, when he heard footsteps on the stairs, in case his dad heard him, and came in to do him.

I keep forgetting, though. His dad was called Jake, like me. He called me Jake, after his dad. He wouldn't have done that if his dad had been a hitter.

He and Steve were mates. I can't believe that. I don't want to know about that. And even if they were then, they wouldn't be now. Not if I told my dad what Steve does to me. He'd be on my side, my dad would. A son's more important than a friend. Any time.

It must be nearly tea-time. I've been in here all day,

with a thumping headache. Mrs Judd's brought me cups of tea and stuff, but mostly I pretended I was asleep so she'd leave me alone.

That's the way I've wanted it. I've got up twice to go to the toilet, and I felt wobbly so I just came back in here and lay down again. When I was in the bathroom, though, I looked out of the window, and saw the drainpipe. My dad is a really, really brave person.

When I woke up early this morning, before I came up here, I was still on the sofa downstairs, but I didn't remember all at once where I was. There was just a chink of light coming through the curtains, and everything looked strange and scary.

Mrs Judd came in on tiptoe, and I remembered everything all at once and shut my eyes again. She looked down at me for ages. I tried not let my eyelids flutter. I think she was having another good look at me, to check if I was really Danny's son. And I thought, maybe she wishes I wasn't. Maybe she's trying to get out of all this.

I couldn't keep my eyes shut for ever, so I opened them and squinted up at her, and she said, 'Awake at last. I'd forgotten about boys, the way they sleep.'

Her voice was almost soft, though she isn't that kind of person, and I felt as if I'd passed a test.

She knows, I thought. She's sure I'm me.

She went to the window and pulled back the curtains. The sun was shining right into the room, so bright it made me screw my eyes up.

'I'll be late for school,' I said, trying to sit up.

She laughed.

'You're not going to school today. It's gone eleven. Anyway, they'd take one look at your face and send for the doctor. Or the police.'

That woke me up even further.

'Where's Mum?' I said, trying to sit up, though I ached all over. It felt funny waking up with all my clothes on. Sweaty and scratchy.

'Out.' She must have seen the fright on my face, because she went on quickly, 'She'll be back, though. She's only gone to work to tell them she'll be off for a day or two.'

'Off? Why? She never takes time off, not for anything.'

'Just till she gets things sorted out. Anyway, it's the first place he'll look for her, isn't it?'

My heart jumped.

'He won't find us here, though, will he? We're safe here. He'll do his nut if he gets on to us. He'll make her go back. She always has to do what he wants in the end. And I'll have to go back too.'

'Over my dead body,' said Mrs Judd.

She sounded angry, but I felt warm all the way through. My breath came out in a great big gust.

She was picking the blankets up off the floor and folding them into perfect little squares.

'I hope you're hungry,' she said. 'There's enough to feed an army in the kitchen.'

The word 'army' gave me the guts I needed.

'Mrs Judd,' I said, swallowing, 'do you think my dad's going to be pleased to see me?'

She didn't answer till she'd put the blankets down on her chair.

'You don't have to say Mrs Judd,' she said. 'You can call me Grandma if you like.'

She didn't sound very sure about it, and to be honest, I wasn't either. I could hardly say the word in my head, never mind out loud. She didn't feel like a grandma. Not yet, anyway.

'Thank you,' I said, and I managed to stand up, and followed her out to the kitchen. She hadn't answered my question, and I didn't feel like asking it again.

I've been asking it all day, though, in my head.

Mum didn't come back till gone five. I was feeling better all of a sudden. My headache had gone, more or less, and I wasn't dizzy any more.

I was back downstairs on the sofa watching TV when she rang on the doorbell. I went to answer it. I checked it was her through the glass pane, though, before I let her in.

'Gawd,' she said, when she saw my face. 'Look at you.'

It's true. My face is even worse than last night, now the bruises are coming out.

She was carrying a supermarket bag in each hand and she put them down to take off her jacket.

'Where have you been all day, Mum?' I was trying to sound cool but I didn't feel it. I'd started to get dead worried. 'He didn't see you, did he? Are you sure he hasn't followed you back here?'

Mrs Judd came out of the kitchen before she had time to answer.

'How did you get on, then?' she asked.

Mum was hanging on to the banister rail with one

hand and easing her shoes off with the other. Her toes looked red and cramped up as if she'd been walking miles, and she was wriggling them in relief.

She put her shoes tidily under the hall table and I looked up and saw an almost approving look in Mrs Judd's face.

'They've got a bloody nerve,' Mum said, picking her bags up and following Mrs Judd into the kitchen. ' "You've made yourself voluntarily homeless, Miss Lindsay. You'll have to take your place in the queue like everyone else." '

She put her bags down on the kitchen table. Mrs Judd had her back to us. She was bending down, looking through the glass door of her oven. A lovely smell of cooking meat was coming out of it.

'Does that mean we've got to go home, then?' I said.

'No.' Mrs Judd straightened up and turned round. 'You're not going near Steve Barlow, either of you.'

She sounded so bossy I could see Mum wanted to say something back just for the heck of it, but she was pleased in a way too. She wasn't used to having someone on her side.

'I've bought chips and stuff for Jake's tea,' she said, beginning to unpack her bags. 'Let me know when it's convenient to use the kitchen. I won't get in your way.'

'What did you go and do that for?' Mrs Judd looked annoyed. 'I've done us a casserole and a crumble for afters. It'll be ready at six. Go and sit in the front room. You look done in. I don't want two crocks on my hands.'

Mum didn't like that.

'We're not going to be on your hands,' she said, flaring up. 'I'm not ungrateful. You've given us a bed and all that, but you don't have to feed us. All I want is to get a place on our own and a chance to get back on my feet. I don't need you or Steve or anyone else.'

What about the baby? I thought, and I could feel my forehead wrinkle up with worry lines. You'll need someone then. I can't help you enough, not on my own. Not with the baby.

'Mum, what about—' I started to say before I could stop myself, but she turned on me like a wildcat.

'What about nothing,' she said. 'Shut up, Jake.'

Mrs Judd had calmly taken Mum's carrier bags off the table and dumped them on the draining board.

'Don't make me laugh, Marie. If anyone ever needed looking after it's you. You always have done but you never got it. More shame to me.'

'That is such crap, excuse my French,' Mum said, angry spots on her cheeks.

'You two came here last night to this house,' Mrs Judd went on, squashing Mum flat as if she was driving the tank in the picture upstairs on my dad's wall, 'like a couple of stray kittens to get what you should have had years ago. Your rights. I'm glad you had the sense to do it, and I'm ashamed of myself for nearly sending you away. But . . .' She stopped, and glared at Mum as if she was deeply offended. 'Now you're here I'm not letting you wander off back out there into all kinds of trouble. Steve Barlow's not coming anywhere near my grandson again, or you for that matter. You're staying with me till you get properly sorted out, with safeguards, and

55

there'll be no more oven-ready chips and chicken nuggets. Look at you. Skin and bones, the pair of you. It's years since I had the chance to do any proper cooking and you're not going to deprive me of it.'

They stared at each other across the kitchen table, and my eyes were going backwards and forwards like when you're watching a tennis match on TV. I knew who'd win. Mum always caved in when she came up against someone strong, and you could no more budge Mrs Judd, my grandma, than the Tower of London.

Mum slumped down on a chair by the table like a cushion that's just lost all its stuffing.

'Yes,' I said, 'but what happens if my dad comes home? Does he ever? Will he soon? What will he think if he finds us here?'

That brought Mum's head up again.

'I know you think that's what I'm after, your darling Danny,' she said, 'but I'm not. Not now. Not ever. I wouldn't touch him with a barge pole. You can tell him that from me, Mrs Judd, next time he gives you a call.'

Mrs Judd sighed, as if she was really irritated.

'For God's sake, you two, I wish you'd stop calling me Mrs Judd. Makes me feel like a perishing land-lady. I'm Grandma to you, Jake; and, Marie, you can call me Doreen.'

Mum said nothing, but I said, 'Yes, Grandma.' And I wasn't going to shut up this time, so I went on, 'I really want to know. Where is my dad? Is he coming home? What will he think about me? Oh, yes, and have I got any brothers and sisters?'

I've always had to make do on scraps of information, little titbits, and it's been like trying to make up one of those big mosaic pictures with only one or two tiny little tiles. There was just that story about how he came to see me in the hospital when I was born, and the letter, and once or twice things Mum let slip. I was like one of those starving famine people you see on the TV, picking little seeds out of the dust to survive.

But now I feel like I'm looking at this totally amazing feast, and the table's cracking up under the weight of mounds and mounds of food and I don't know where to start. Just looking at it all gives me indigestion.

Mrs Judd got started while she was dishing out her casserole, and she didn't stop till we'd polished off the crumble.

I could see Mum didn't like it much at first. She's never wanted to talk about my dad. And the way Mrs Judd was going on about him made her tighten her mouth till it was a straight line across her face.

The thing is, I reckon, that Danny is a one-track mind thing with Mrs Judd. She may be mad with him at the moment, on account of the way he ditched Mum and me, but she forgot about that once she got started.

'Can't say I was all that keen on him going into the army,' she began. 'There was the danger, and from what you hear, the bullying and all that. But it got him away from home and . . .' She stopped.

'And from going with bad company. Me for instance,' said Mum, her face reddening.

'All right, yes.' Mrs Judd isn't one to duck things

when they come right at her. 'I'll admit it. I'm not saying I shouldn't have seen things differently, with regard to you, though at the time . . . But there was Steve too. Very glad, I was, to see the back of him. And you can't say I wasn't right about that.'

'Steve's got his points,' Mum said. 'It wasn't all . . .'

Then she saw me looking at her, and she stopped.

'The army did a lot for Danny,' Mrs Judd said, her voice all fond again. 'Got him a good training. REME. Royal Electrical and Mechanical Engineers, that's what he was in. Travelled all over the world – Germany, Belize, Falklands, Kenya – and he was in the Gulf War too.'

'Was he in a battle?' I said. 'Did he have to shoot guns and let off bombs and stuff?'

'It was more the vehicle maintenance side of things. Repairing tanks. Servicing trucks. Keeping everything in trim.' She picked up the salt and pepper and put them tidily side by side, bang in the middle of the table. 'Essential work on the supply side.'

'Safe and easy, you mean,' said Mum. 'Never was much of a one for getting himself hurt, Danny. Drainpipe or no drainpipe.'

'Or hurting other people,' I said hopefully, but I don't think either of them heard me.

'Oh, there's plenty of danger in REME,' Mrs Judd said, sounding annoyed. 'In the Gulf they had all sorts. Bombs flying about, mines, explosions, you name it.'

'What about this wife of his, then?' Mum said, looking at the piece of meat she was cutting up as if that was the only thing she was interested in. 'I suppose she swans off to Africa and Germany and wherever with him.'

'Sandra? Ha!' Mrs Judd speared a piece of potato with a jab of her fork. 'Ran off with a lance corporal, didn't she? All over Danny like suntan oil one day, dirty little slut, trying to get money out of him, then off to spend it with one of Danny's own platoon mates the next. He went AWOL, did Mr Lance Corporal. They got him though. Banged him up in the glasshouse for a bit. Sandra left him soon after, but she never went back to Danny. Good riddance, as far as I'm concerned.'

'But what about the kids?' I said. 'Their family?'

'What family?'

'Mum, you said, every time I asked you, he'd got another family. That means kids, doesn't it?'

Mum shrugged.

'I thought he did have. Last I'd heard he'd got this Sandra up the duff.'

'Who told you that?' Mrs Judd looked upset.

'Barney. That friend of Steve's who used to go around with him and Danny. Danny wrote to him sometimes. He sent a letter to me through Barney once.'

'So what happened to the baby?' I asked.

'Sandra had an abortion, that's what.' Mrs Judd shuddered and put her knife and fork down. 'Didn't even tell Danny till afterwards. Little Miss Me-First. "I'm not saddling myself with a screaming kid. I want to live my own life. So you know where you can get off, Danny, and your old mum who's dying to be a grandma." '

'You mean,' I said, wanting to make sure I'd got

this really straight, 'that I haven't got any brothers and sisters at all? That I'm the only one?'

Mrs Judd put out her leathery old hand and touched mine.

'You are. My only grandchild. And when I think how I missed out on it all, taking you out in your pram, and feeding the ducks in the park, and seeing you in your nativity play at school, I feel really sick.'

'*You* feel sick?' Mum said sarcastically. 'Never mind the bleeding ducks. You could have got him out of Steve's way when things went bad and I didn't have the guts to face up to what was happening.'

They'd both worked themselves into a corner and stopped talking. Mrs Judd got up and cleared the plates away and fetched the crumble out of the oven.

'You said he's in Lancashire now,' I said. 'What's the army doing in Lancashire? There isn't a war on there, is there?'

'Oh, Danny's not in the army now,' said Mrs Judd, and one of the few pieces of my mosaic came unhitched and went flying off into nothingness. 'He's on motorway construction. Earthworks foreman on the M6 upgrade.'

She sounded proud. Mum laughed.

'Road building? Shovelling dirt on a motorway? Bit of a comedown for you, isn't it, Doreen, with his dad running his own shop and all?'

'My grandad had a shop?' I said, feeling as if I was being buffeted from one side to the other.

'My Jake had a nice little shoe business on the high street. Yes,' Mrs Judd went on. 'He wanted Danny to take it on but it was always going to be the big picture for Danny. I could see that from very early on.'

The big picture. I liked that. Foreign travel. Tanks and heavy vehicles and convoys. Earthworks and motorways and tunnels and bridges.

'When's he coming home, then?' I said.

'Well, this isn't exactly his home any more,' Mrs Judd said regretfully. 'He's got a place of his own up Preston way. He's out on the roads, though, most of the time. Doesn't get more than one weekend in three off. I never know when he's coming down here. He likes to surprise me, Danny does. There's a knock on the door one day and there he is, with a bag of laundry in one hand and a box of Quality Street in the other. They don't change, Marie. You'll find that out when Jake's older. Whatever Danny's done, and I'm not proud of him at the moment, I'm still his mum and I always will be.'

And I'm his son and I always have been, I thought.

But now that I'm back here, lying in his bed, I'm beginning to wonder if I'm right. The picture of my dad that I carry in my head has grown up with me. It's always been a part of me. Whatever Steve did to me, it never went away. Actually, it got more and more important.

I can see now that it was all wrong. The face I've dreamed up at night before I've gone to sleep, the man I've called out for in my heart when I was so scared I thought I was done for – he's never been real at all.

There's no one in a scarlet tunic with gold stripes on his arms and a couple of kids climbing on his knees. There probably never was a red uniform, and there wasn't even one baby.

Instead, there's a fuzzy photo of a man in khaki overalls standing in the shadow of a tank (I was right about that bit, anyway. Mrs Judd said he was the one at the back), and an earthworks foreman, whatever that means.

But I can't see him at all. The face that was as real to me as my own has disappeared and in its place there's nothing. There's no one there at all.

I can't stay off school for ever, and it'll take weeks for my face to go back to normal. Anyway, I've been on my own in the house with Mrs Judd for three days now, and I'm starting to go potty.

It's not that I don't like her. I do. There's lots of good things about her, like the way she stands up for herself, and the way she sticks up for my dad, as if she was a big mamma dog with one naughty puppy. She's strong, and kind at the same time. Solid. I like that.

I like it best when she talks about my dad. I get her to tell me things all the time.

The best bits are about all the things he did when he was my age. Once he stuck two massive Brazil nuts into his nose, so that one dangled down out of each nostril, and waited to see how long it would be before anyone noticed. He kept on coming into the kitchen, where Mrs Judd was cooking, and going outside to where his dad was fixing the gate, and they kept on not looking at him.

In the end, they were all sitting round the table for their tea, and Mrs Judd said, 'Eat your fish pie,

Danny, what's the matter with you?' and they still hadn't noticed anything. And there was this laugh building up inside my dad, building and building, and it came bursting out. And one of the Brazil nuts shot across the table and pinged on the pie dish, and the other one dropped into Mr Judd's cup of tea. And Mr Judd said, 'Mother, where did this Brazil nut come from?' and they both looked up at the ceiling, as if nuts were raining down from on high. And my dad, when he got over laughing, said, 'That just proves it. I could turn into an Eskimo, and you'd never know the difference.'

But it's kind of tiring being around Mrs Judd for too long. She keeps fetching me things to eat, like she was fattening me up for Christmas. You can see she's not used to other people being in her house. It fusses her. She picks up the cushions after I've got up from the sofa and plumps them up again, and she follows me halfway up the stairs to remind me about not tripping up on the loose rug at the top.

Maybe all grandmas are like Mrs Judd. Perhaps grandads are too. If ever I get to be a grandad, that's probably what I'll be like.

Mum doesn't want me to go back to school yet. She keeps saying they'll be on to me, and she hasn't spent all these years ducking and diving and keeping her head down, to keep me out of care, only to have them whip me off her and stick me in a children's home now.

Sometimes, when it's been really bad with Steve, I've wished she hadn't been so careful. I don't know if I wouldn't rather have been in a children's home, sometimes. When she talks about Willowbank, where she was, it doesn't sound that bad. They had a lot of laughs, the way she tells it, and the person who ran it, Auntie Jean, was really nice.

I'd have been miserable without Mum, though. I know that. Especially when I was younger. Steve's always knocked me about, ever since I can remember, and her too, a bit, but he wasn't like this, he wasn't murderous, till a couple of years ago, after I got so tall.

I had a go at Mum about school this morning, till she gave in.

'I'll tell them I fell off my bike,' I said. 'It worked with Kieran. Anyway, I've always got round it before. They never see my bruises. When it's PE I change in the corner, where it's dark.'

She bit her lip then, and Mrs Judd, who was listening, frowned so hard her big black brows met in the middle.

'Anyway,' I said, 'if I don't go back today, we'll have to get a doctor's letter or they'll send the truant officer round, have you thought of that?'

The best thing about going back to school was the first bit, just getting out of the house and running down the road on my own. I'd started to feel like a prisoner in Mrs Judd's house.

I had a narrow escape, though. Mum had gone off to work first, and Mrs Judd said, 'You don't know your way to school, do you, Jake? I'd better come with you. Wait while I lock up the back door.'

I said, really quickly, 'It's OK. I've been round this way loads of times. I know where to go, honestly,' and I picked up my bag and made a dash for it, out of the house and down the street, before she could turn around.

I got lost at once, of course. But it didn't matter because there were loads of kids wearing my school uniform on the main street, down at the bottom of Sunnybrook Road, where Mrs Judd's house is, so I just followed them.

When I got near the school gate I stopped and had a good look round, in case Steve was hanging about, but I didn't see him, so I went on in.

I was worried, though, by how everyone kept on about my face. It was things like, 'Wow, Jake, what does the other guy look like?' and, 'When's the next big fight, Jake? Can we come and watch?'

I kept saying, 'Fell off my bike. Ran into a tree, didn't I.'

Luckily I bumped into Kieran first thing, and he went around with me all through break and lunch-time, as if I was a kind of star and he was my minder, and he said to them all, 'Yeah, you should have seen the bike. It's a write-off.'

Mrs McLeish was the nosy one. She was the one that worried me. She kept me behind after English.

'What happened to your face, Jake?' she said, looking all concerned, as if she was a nurse or something.

'Fell off my bike, Miss,' I said.

'What? Speak up. I can't hear you.'

'Ran my bike into a tree. It was my fault. Wasn't looking where I was going.'

She was fiddling with her necklace.

'Everything all right at home, Jake? You live with

65

your mum and your stepfather, don't you? Do you get along with him all right? With your stepfather?'

I shrugged. This was a mistake because it hurt the whacking great bruise I'd still got on my ribs, and she noticed.

'He's OK. Can I go now, Miss?'

'What happened to your bike?' She was looking at me all the time, really hard, and I could feel my hands start to go sweaty.

'Write-off, wasn't it, Miss,' I said. 'All mashed up.'

'So what did you do with it?'

I wasn't ready for this.

'What do you mean?' I was trying to think.

'I mean, Jake, what did you do with your bike?'

'I left it there, beside the road.'

'What about the bits on it, I mean, didn't you have a D-lock on it, or a front lamp? Did you just leave those on it too?'

I was feeling the pressure now.

'Don't know, Miss. I don't remember. My head felt funny.'

'I bet it did.' She was sounding really sympathetic, but it felt threatening to me. 'What did the doctor say?'

'I didn't go.' I couldn't look at her, and I just kept licking my lips. 'Mum said I needed time off in bed, that was all.'

'I see.' She was nodding her head, up and down, like a bleeding mechanical toy. 'I'll give your mum a ring. Just to check everything's OK.'

'No!' I had a picture in my head, like a flash, of the phone ringing in our flat, and Steve picking it up, and all hell breaking loose. 'You can't phone Mum. She'll be at work.'

'After work, then,' she said. 'It's OK, Jake. Look, it's nothing to worry about. I just want to make sure you're all right, that's all.'

'We've moved house,' I said, trying to keep the panic out of my voice. 'We're staying with my grandma. She's not very well. We're looking after her. She's not to be bothered. There's no one in our flat. My stepdad's gone away. I don't know where he is.'

'Right.' She was looking dead suspicious, and I knew I'd said too much. 'What's your grandma's name, Jake? What's her phone number?'

'She's not on the phone.' I was feeling really desperate. 'Got cut off last week.'

'What's her address, then? You must know where you're living. You must know your grandma's name.'

I had another flash, a picture of Mrs Judd standing on the doorstep of her house, with her arms folded across her chest, and Mrs McLeish and a couple of policemen trying to force their way past her to get in and take me away.

But she wouldn't let them, I thought. She'd see them off. She'd send the lot of them packing, and I felt this stupid grin spreading across my face.

'My grandma's name is Mrs Judd,' I said, 'and she lives at 16 Sunnybrook Road.'

All this stuff with Mrs McLeish got me worried, and that made me careless. I forgot Steve might be waiting around after school. Earlier on, I'd planned how I'd go out of school by the back way, down by the brewery, and work up to the main road through the side streets, but it was such a habit, going out of the main entrance, that I did it without thinking. There I was, walking out of the big front gates with my head down, hands in pockets, not even noticing everyone else rushing past me, when I ran smack into him.

I tell you, it was one of the worst moments of my life.

Everything inside me went still and I thought I was going to pass out. Then my heart gave this powerful kick, like an animal was jumping inside my chest, and my knees began to shake.

I tried, in a stupid, weak kind of way to dodge past him, but he just moved sideways and blocked me. Quick on his feet, is Steve. I've never been able to get away from him. I knew I wouldn't this time, so I gave up trying.

'Come with me, you.'

He took my arm and tried to pull me away, up the road. My eyes were darting around, looking for a way out, and I saw Mrs McLeish by the school gate. She was standing there with Mr Grossmith, the head of PE. They were staring in our direction. I saw her point me out to him, and Mr Grossmith started staring at us too. They made me feel a little bit braver.

'Can't,' I said. 'Just remembered. I've got football practice. I've got to go back in.'

'Football? Since when did you know how to kick a football?'

His voice had the edge in it that I dreaded.

I didn't say anything else, I couldn't, but I went on

looking towards Mrs McLeish and Mr Grossmith and Steve turned his head too, and saw them watching us. He dropped his hand off my arm at once and took a step backwards, then he ran his fingers through his hair and looked at me in a different way, as if he was seeing me properly for the first time.

'What happened to your face?' he said. 'Ran into a bus?'

I couldn't believe it. He'd beaten my head in and half killed me and probably scarred me for life and he'd blanked it out. Just like that.

I didn't say anything. I stood there and looked at him.

A weird thing happened then. For the first time ever I saw something like shame in Steve's face. Or it could have been regret. It was over in a flash.

'I only want to talk to you,' he said, and it was almost as if there was a whine in his voice. 'I only want to know where she is.'

I was getting worried because the flow of people coming out of the gates was slowing down. In a minute they'd all be round the corner, at the bus stops, and Mrs McLeish and Mr Grossmith would go back inside the gates and I'd be alone with him.

I'd been backing away slowly, and then I saw my chance. A bunch of loudmouths from the year above me were coming up behind me, pulling the straps of each others' bags and doing headlocks and football type tackles. I zipped round behind them and got back in through the school gates while they were all dodging about in Steve's way.

I heard him shout, 'No one ever runs out on me,

do you hear me? No one!' But I didn't look back. I was racing off down the side of the games field.

Mr Grossmith was calling after me now.

'Jake? Where are you going? Come here, Jake!'

I stopped for him. I didn't want to, but I reckoned he'd start nosing around me tomorrow if I didn't. Anyway, I like Mr Grossmith.

'Left my sweatshirt on the steps outside the library, sir,' I said. 'Can I go now, sir?'

I didn't wait for an answer. I made a quick detour round in front of the library, in case he was watching, then I legged it under the cover of the trees at the edge of the field to the back gate. It was locked, of course. It always is, but you can get over it in half a second if you put one foot on the crossbar and take care with the barbed wire running along the top.

It took me a good ten minutes to get back up to the main road, and I felt safe all that time. I knew Steve couldn't have followed me. But once I was out on the shopping street, with crowds of people going past and buses running up and down, I wasn't so sure. I had that funny feeling, that prickly weird feeling, that eyes were on me. Following me.

I went into a newsagent and stood just inside the door and watched the street for a long time, pretending I was waiting for someone. I didn't see anything. There wasn't even anyone out there in the street who looked like Steve.

I guessed I'd been imagining things, and I walked on quickly, back to Mrs Judd's.

I never used to think about families, about being in one, and what it would be like, but now I've got a grandma and a real dad, even if he's only in a photograph, it's kind of set me off. It makes things complicated because you have to make room for more people in your mind. I'd better get used to it because when the baby comes, there'll be another new person, and there'll be a whole lot more stuff that's going to happen.

I was scared before, when I thought about the baby. I don't know what I feel now.

My dream house has changed, anyway. The tower's still there, in case I need it, but I won't have my bed in it. There's going to be more like an ordinary house, but big and beautiful, special and different. There'll easily be enough space for the four of us, for my mum and dad and the baby and me. Because we'd all be living in it together, like a real family.

I'd have a brilliant room of course, with loads of stuff, all the things I could ever want. And there'd be a big window looking out across the strip of sea towards the land, because we'd still be on an island. Oh, yes, that's good, the island idea.

My mum and dad would have the same bedroom, a big one, with white furniture and huge windows to let all the sunshine in. And my baby sister would have a little room off theirs, with the sorts of things she'd like, teddies and flowery stuff and everything pink.

We'd go out together in the evening, when the parrots fly above the forest, to watch the chimps and gorillas, and Mum and Dad would hold hands, and I'd carry the baby, and I'd pick the golden apples for her as the sun went down.

71

Mrs Judd would live nearby, not too close, in a little guardhouse by the jetty where the boats come in. Her chair (the one with the wooden arms) would be pulled up near a window so she could watch out and see who was trying to get on to the island. She'd send them away if she didn't like the look of them.

She'd have her pots and pans too, and a great big kitchen. On Sundays we'd go down to her place and she'd cook us a slap-up roast with all the trimmings. And one of her crumbles for afters.

We'd just finished our supper (bangers and mash with ice cream to follow) when the knock came on the door. Mrs Judd had gone into the toilet, as it happened, so Mum answered it. I knew, in the second before she opened it, who would be standing there, and I called out, 'Don't, Mum! Wait!' But I was too late.

Steve had been in the pub. His face was red and I could smell the beer on his breath from halfway down the hall. I wanted to turn round and dash out through the kitchen and out of the back door, but I didn't. I could see that Mum was sort of shrivelling up, going weak and soft like she always did with Steve. I was afraid he'd twist her round his finger again and I knew I couldn't just run away and let it happen.

Steve didn't say anything for a moment. He just stood there, staring at Mum, balling his fists and tightening his jaw till I could see all the muscles in his neck standing out like ropes.

'Slag. You slag.' His voice wasn't slurred. He wasn't pissed, just a bit tanked up, enough to make him even nastier than usual. 'Where is he? Get him out here.'

Mum was trying to stiffen herself, and when she spoke her voice came out high and squeaky.

'Piss off, Steve. We're out of it, Jake and me. You nearly killed him.' She turned and grabbed my arm, and hauled me out on to the step beside her. 'Look at that. Look at what you did to his face. Bloody psycho. I've had enough.'

She tried to shut the door. Steve stuck his foot in it. He wasn't looking at me.

'Not him. Lover boy. Your lover boy. Danny. Where's Danny?'

'Danny?' Mum tossed her head back. 'Him? I haven't seen him since he dumped me. Don't care if I never see him again. And that goes for you too.'

Steve lunged forward, shoved the door wide open, grabbed her by the shoulders and started shaking her.

I was crying now, feeling as helpless as a baby, just standing there, clawing uselessly at his arm. He kicked out sideways and caught me on my shin with the toe of his boot. I staggered back down the hall.

'Mrs Judd!' I yelled. 'Grandma! Come quick. Steve's killing my mum!'

The toilet flushed upstairs and Mrs Judd came out. She walked down the stairs at her usual speed, drying her hands on a towel.

Steve saw her and his face changed. He was still holding Mum, but he wasn't shaking her any more.

'Stop that, Steven,' Mrs Judd said. 'Let go of Marie. You ought to be ashamed of yourself.'

She sounded like a teacher ticking off a five-year-old kid. Steve dropped his hands.

'Hiding him, are you, your precious Danny?' He was trying to sound hard but he wasn't so sure of himself now. 'Under the bed, is he? I'm coming in. I'm going to kill him.'

I was still hopping about clutching my shin, but I was starting to feel a bit less scared. Mrs Judd went to stand beside Mum, making Steve drop back off the doorstep.

'You're not setting foot in this house, Steven Barlow,' she said.

She wasn't shouting or anything. She was calm and sort of solid.

He won't go for her, I thought. He won't dare, and a bubble of confidence started growing in my chest.

'Get him out here, then,' said Steve. 'Send Danny out. Is he scared, or what?'

'He's not here,' I said, the bubble growing bigger. 'My dad's up north.'

'Your what?' The scorn in his eyes almost scorched me. The bubble burst and I stepped back.

'He is my dad,' I managed to say. 'Mrs Judd knows it now. She knows she's my grandma.'

He spat on the path.

'She can keep you. Good riddance.'

I'd made things worse, I could see that. He was tensing himself up again as if he was going to push past her. Mrs Judd crossed her arms over her chest and leaned against the doorpost.

'GBH,' she said. 'Assault and battery. On a minor. It counts as child abuse. Quite a long sentence, I should think.'

Steve eyes seemed to bulge as he stared at her.

'Where's Danny?' His voice grated as if his throat was lined with sandpaper.

'Up north, like Jake said. He doesn't know they're here. He's not going to like what you've done to his son.'

'Ha!' Steve stabbed a finger towards her. 'You think Danny gives a monkey's? Pushed off, didn't he, the minute the kid was born, so he wouldn't have to do the maintenance. His son! Not even a fiver in the post at Christmas.'

I shut my eyes. This was the dark place in my mind where I didn't want to go. The thought I'd been trying not to think. It felt like a dagger in my ribs.

Mrs Judd was flummoxed too. She hesitated. Steve saw it, and took hold of Mum's arm. He was trying to yank her off the doorstep.

'You're coming with me.'

She'd always done what he said before. I was dead scared she'd do it again. I caught her other hand and pulled at it.

'No, Mum. You can't. Please, Mum. Don't.'

She shook us both off.

'Get out, you bastard. You come back here again and I'll do you for child abuse, like she said.'

Mrs Judd nodded, as if she was satisfied. If she'd been someone else, without standards, she'd have shown him two fingers. She began to shut the door.

'You can't do this, Marie!' Steve shouted. He'd dropped all his loud talk and sounded in a panic. 'It's my baby. You're going to have my baby!'

'Jake,' Mrs Judd said to me over her shoulder. 'I'm not standing for harassment at my own front door a minute longer. Dial 999 and get the police. I'm pressing charges on you, Steven Barlow, unless you get off my premises this instant and leave us in peace.'

She shut the door. I dodged past her and Mum and ran upstairs to look out of my bedroom window, though I didn't pull the nets back because I didn't want him to see me. He was standing at the gate, looking up at the house, his face murderous. If he'd had a bazooka in his hand he'd have blown us all sky high, then and there. But he didn't. He just went off down the road.

I sat down on the bed. I was shaking, as if I'd just escaped from certain death. I needed something to do, and anyway, I wanted to know if Mrs Judd had dialled 999, so I went back to the top of the stairs. Mrs Judd seemed to have forgotten about the police. She was standing right in front of Mum, who was leaning against the front door with her hands behind her back.

'Now then, Marie,' Mrs Judd was saying. 'What's all this about a baby?'

I didn't hang around to hear what happened next. I was afraid there'd be a bit of a ding dong, and that's what I hate.

Loud voices. People shouting. Anger.

I went back into his bedroom (my room now) and I shut the door.

We did it, I thought, and I punched the air with my hand. We saw him off!

I'd got into a bit of a habit, since I'd been at Mrs Judd's, of talking to the photo of my dad, the one of him in the shadows, behind the tank. I looked at it now. I was going to tell him about what we'd done. Instead I heard myself saying, 'You ducked out. You never even sent me a fiver at Christmas.'

It was horrible. I couldn't understand myself. I'd never been angry with my dad before, but now I was. Really, really angry.

'You left us,' I said. 'You didn't care. You let Steve beat me up, on and on, beating me up. You never came to see if I was OK. You never sent a fiver at Christmas.'

I could feel the tears pricking inside my eyelids, but I wasn't going to cry. I wasn't going to give him the satisfaction.

'We don't need you now anyway,' I told the picture. 'We're going to get shot of Steve and get out of here. Find a place of our own. We're better off without anyone, Mum and me.'

But I didn't mean that. I didn't want to be without Mrs Judd again. It wasn't only that she was our protector, sort of, or that we were living in her house. I'd got used to her. I'd started to really like her.

'Your mum's worth ten of you,' I told my dad.

I stopped then. I didn't want to go on and say worse things. I didn't want to lose the good feeling I'd always had, deep inside myself, that I'd find him one day and he'd make everything right for me.

'The jury's out on you,' I told him. 'For now.'

I didn't want to stay in the room any longer. I opened the door and listened. They were in the kitchen, talking. Their voices sounded quiet and normal. I went downstairs and into the kitchen.

'Like I said, Marie, you should have trusted me,' Mrs Judd was saying. 'You didn't really think I'd throw you out, did you? And put that fag out. It's bad for the baby.'

Mum looked up at me as I came in. She looked half relieved, half trapped, like a little kid who's been caught out doing something dangerous and is secretly glad to be rescued.

'You knew about all this, I suppose?' Mrs Judd frowned at me.

'Yes. She said not to tell.' A bit of the anger I'd felt upstairs seemed to be coming out again, I didn't know why. 'Why should she? We won't be here when it's born. We'll be sorted out by then.'

Mrs Judd looked hurt.

'Oh, pardon me. It's none of my business. Suit yourselves.'

I felt sorry.

'I didn't mean—' I began.

She turned her back on us and started filling the kettle at the sink.

I bit my lip and exchanged a look with Mum.

'Look, Doreen,' Mum said, stubbing out her cigarette. 'It's just that you've done a lot for us, you know?'

Mrs Judd plugged the kettle in, turned round and wagged a finger at her.

'That's where you're wrong. Nothing. I've done nothing! Every bruise on that child's body' – she nodded in my direction – 'is a reproach. It keeps me awake at night thinking about what he's suffered. I can't make it up to you, but you might at least let me try.'

Mum did something awful then. She put her arms

on the table, put her head down on them and burst into tears.

Mrs Judd sat down beside her and started shoving tissues into her hands.

'Silly girl,' she said. 'Now let's get this straight. How far gone are you? Have you started at the antenatal? Take off those high-heeled shoes, for God's sake, or your ankles will blow up like balloons.'

That was enough for me. I left them to it. Went out and closed the door, and switched on the telly in the front room. So much had happened it was doing my head in and I knew it would take a couple of soaps and a quiz show to calm me down.

I don't know why Kieran likes going round with me. There are loads of people at school who are really popular, and a lot more fun than me. He could have been best mates with any of them.

I haven't been much of a one for friends up to now. Friends make things complicated. You have to tell things to friends. They want to come to your house, and look through your stuff, and show you all theirs.

But Kieran's different. He came that day, when I'd nearly topped myself, and I'd seen the baby on the train, and everything in the world was suddenly precious and beautiful. He'd been like a present.

'Hello, puff-face,' he said. He was hanging round the door to the cloakroom as if he was waiting for me. 'Your eyes have gone down a bit today, though. And your nose. I won't be able to call you that much longer.'

'Kieran! You on for football?' Greg called out. He was jumping up and down on the edge of the sports field, keeping the ball in the air with his feet and knees.

'In a minute,' Kieran called back. He turned to me again. 'When are you coming back to our base? There's stuff we could do there. I've been thinking.'

Our base, I thought. He called it ours. I didn't mind. I quite liked it. But the place seemed long ago and miles away now. As if I'd moved into another life.

The ball came whizzing at him before I'd thought of an answer. He whammed it back to Greg.

'I'm not sure,' I said. 'I'm staying with my grandma. She's on the other side, past the bus station. Up Sunnybrook Road.'

He looked surprised.

'It's posh up there. How long are you staying? Have your mum and dad gone away?'

I took a deep breath. This was getting dangerous. I wasn't used to telling people things, especially people at school.

'My dad's up north.'

I stopped. He didn't say anything. I could see he was waiting for me to go on.

Friends don't keep secrets, I told myself. Not big ones.

'Me and my mum,' I said, feeling almost breathless, as if I'd been running a race, 'we've moved in with my dad's mum. My mum and my stepdad have split up.'

'Oh.'

He didn't sound impressed.

'Was it because of the bike that he duffed you up?'

'Who said anyone duffed me up?'

'Jake, I'm not thick. I saw him. That day. I saw you hide too. You looked like you'd just busted out from Death Row.'

That made me laugh.

'I had. That's just where I'd busted out from.'

I wanted to tell him things then, about Mum, and Steve, and Mrs Judd and the baby. Even about my dad. I would have done, too, if Greg hadn't come up again and gone on about playing football. And then the bell went, and there was registration, and I just slipped back into the person I always am at school, the quiet one who does what he's told and never gets into trouble, the one who slips unnoticed down the corridor, the one who never listens to a word the teachers say (if only they knew), but stares out of the window or up at the ceiling and keeps his thoughts to himself.

I always change for PE in the darkest corner of the cloakroom. That way, no one will see me without my clothes on. There won't be any tricky questions. No sympathy. No prying. Nobody being nosy.

Mr Grossmith doesn't usually bother with us while we're changing. He only comes in when he thinks we're taking too long, and he blows his whistle and yells out, 'Come on, you lot. Move it. We haven't got all day.'

But this time he was right there, in the cloakroom, standing in my corner. I looked round for somewhere else to go, but it was awkward. There was nowhere even halfway private. I went as far away from the window as I could, and got my football shirt and shorts out of my bag, so they'd be all ready, and I looked round, and I couldn't see Mr Grossmith. So I whipped my school shirt off and picked my football shirt up.

Mr Grossmith must have come up without me seeing him, because he was suddenly standing right there beside me.

'Turn round, Jake,' he said.

I didn't have any choice. I had to.

He looked at my back for what felt like ages. Then he said, in a different voice, 'You're excused PE today. Go along to the library. I'll come and see you at the end of the lesson.'

I don't think anyone else saw my back, except for Kieran. I know he did because there was a funny look in his eyes when I'd put my school shirt on again, as if he was sympathetic but embarrassed at the same time.

'Lucky you,' was all he said. 'I wouldn't mind a nice little skive in the library. See you at break. I've got an extra Mars bar in my bag if you're interested.'

It was quiet in the library. I fetched a magazine off the rack, and sat behind a bookshelf, and flipped through the pages. Mrs McLeish came in at one point. I saw her between the shelves. She seemed to be looking for someone. I kept still, and she didn't notice me. She went out and I had the place to myself again.

I needed to think. I didn't know what I was going to say to Mr Grossmith. He was on to me, I could tell. What if I told him the truth, and he got the social workers in, and they took me away? But why would they do that, now I wasn't living with Steve any more?

The thing was, Mum had conditioned me for so long, not to let on about anything to anyone, that it was like a habit. An instinct. She'd never said as much, not in so many words, but I knew what she thought.

Keep your head down. Don't say a word. They'll say they're trying to help you, but all you'll get is trouble.

Now, though, it was time for me to think it all out for myself.

GBH, Mrs Judd had said. Child abuse. Prison.

Steve in prison. I felt a prickle of shame at the thought, but a dark joy too. I could do that to him. I could stand up for myself and shop him. I could get him put away, and then I'd be safe and free.

What if he did end up inside, though? He wouldn't be in for long. What would he do to me when he got out?

I was still sitting there, turning the pages of the magazine, not seeing a thing, when Mr Grossmith touched my shoulder. I hadn't heard him coming.

He sat down beside me. He had that concerned look, that busybody, I-know-what's-best-for-you look that made me shrink away from him like a tortoise pulling its head back into its shell.

'Those are very nasty injuries on your back, Jake.'

'Yes, sir. Like I told Mrs McLeish, I fell off my bike.'

'Maybe you did, but that's not how you got those bruises.'

I was still leafing through the magazine. He took it out of my hands and pushed it to the far side of the table.

83

'Who did it, Jake? Who beat you up?'

I said nothing.

'I shall have to report this.'

I was starting to feel trapped.

'Why? It's no one's business. I'm all right, sir, really I am.'

'It is our business. Your welfare is our business. Are you being bullied at school? Is that it? Are you scared that if you tell they'll go for you again?'

I shook my head.

'No one goes for me at school. They leave me alone.'

'Mrs McLeish says you've moved in with your grandma. Why did you do that, Jake? Why did you and your mum leave home?'

I felt my face go red. Things were slipping out of my control.

Interfering cow, I thought. Why doesn't she keep things to herself?

'That was your stepfather who met you after school yesterday, wasn't it?'

Mr Grossmith's voice was soft.

'What if it was, sir?'

'Mrs McLeish said you'd told her he'd gone away.'

'Must have come back then.'

'Jake.' Mr Grossmith put his hand flat down on the table, then lifted it to scratch his head. 'I can't make you tell me things you don't want to, but like I said, I have to report this. It's a legal requirement.'

'You mean you'll get the Social in even if I don't say anything?'

'Don't say it like that. They're only there to help you. We all are.'

I heard the library door open and close, then I saw Kieran. He'd guessed exactly which corner of the library I'd be sitting in. He'd come straight to me. Mr Grossmith had his back to him, and he didn't see him coming.

'You OK, Jake?' Kieran said over Mr Grossmith's head. He didn't care about teachers. They never bothered him. 'I didn't know you'd hurt your back till I saw it. I thought it was only your ugly mug. Is he OK, sir?'

'Yes, Kieran. Go away.' Mr Grossmith didn't even turn round.

'He's my mate,' I said. 'I don't mind him being here.'

'It's amazing how hurt you get in a bicycle accident,' Kieran said. I could see he was trying to help me. He was guessing what I wanted him to say. 'He smashed his bike into a tree.'

'There wasn't a bicycle, was there, Jake? There wasn't a tree, either.' Mr Grossmith's voice was as smooth as silk.

'There was, sir,' Kieran butted in eagerly. 'Jake told me. He—'

I suddenly felt very, very tired.

'No,' I said. 'There wasn't a bicycle and there wasn't a tree. It was Steve. My stepfather. He beat me up.'

I saw, in one quick glance, that Kieran was watching me with a worried look on his face, but then I was looking down at Mr Grossmith's hands, and he was turning a pencil round and round, waiting for me to go on. The light glanced off it and I felt almost hypnotized.

'Why?' Mr Grossmith prompted me. 'Why did he beat you up, Jake?'

'We went to the zoo, him and me and my mum. A monkey peed on him and I laughed.'

I could see Kieran jerk, as if he was going to laugh too, but he didn't.

'It wasn't the first time he'd gone for you, was it?' said Mr Grossmith.

I shut my eyes and shook my head as awful memories, one after the other, of pain and terror surged up into my mind. I was suddenly scared I would cry.

I cleared my throat.

'It won't be the last time, either,' I said, 'if he hears I've grassed him up. Especially if my mum goes back to him. Don't tell anyone, please, sir.'

But I knew he would, and I didn't care any more. Later on, when Mum found out, she'd give me stick for it, maybe.

Only maybe she won't, I thought, remembering how she'd stood up to Steve on the doorstep last night.

Anyway, whatever might happen now, the secret was out. I'd shopped him. I'd done it. I might regret it later on, but right now I felt almost dizzy with relief, and the sweet smell of triumph filled my nostrils.

Kieran walked halfway home with me. It was in the wrong direction for him. He usually got the bus back down towards the railway bridge, near the flats, but he said he wanted to go to the model shop at my end of the high street. I knew he was just doing it so he could look out for me.

I was glad. The minute I got out of school, the powerful feeling left me and I was really scared about what I'd done. I couldn't work out if I was glad or sorry.

Mum opened the door when I got back to Mrs Judd's house. My heart skipped a beat. She didn't usually get off work till five.

'What happened?' I said. 'Why are you back early?'

She made a funny face and jerked her head towards the kitchen door.

'She got me an appointment at the doctor's. They gave me time off for it at work.'

'Are you OK? You're not ill or anything?'

'No. Just a check-up. For the baby.'

The phone rang on the table in the hall. Mrs Judd came out of the kitchen, dusting flour off her hands, and picked it up.

'For you,' she said, giving it to Mum.

Mum backed away and put her hand up.

'I'm not talking to him. Just tell him to leave us alone.'

'It's not Steve. It's Jake's school.'

'Oh.'

She looked worried, and took the phone from Mrs Judd's hand. My blood had turned to ice. The muddle in my head cleared away and I knew I'd done a terrible thing, the worst thing in Mum's book.

The person on the other end of the phone was a woman. She was speaking quietly, going on and on. Mum was hardly saying anything, just, 'Yes,' and 'No,' in a tight flat voice. Every now and then she started to say 'It's not—' or 'I didn't—' but the voice at the other end interrupted her and she shut up.

I sat down on the bottom step of the stairs and tried to think about what I was going to say to her, but the blood was hammering round in my head and I couldn't get my thoughts straight.

I was used to getting it from Steve. I'd learned long ago to guard my mind from him. But when she was angry with me and said things, it hurt all the way down.

She put the receiver back.

'Mum, I couldn't help it. It was Mr Grossmith. He sneaked up on me in the cloakroom. He saw my back. I didn't want to say anything. He stopped me doing PE, then afterwards he went on and on at me. I kept telling him I'd crashed a bike but he didn't believe me. Mum, I'm sorry. He got it out of me. I didn't mean to say anything. Mum, you've got to believe me.'

'That was the social services,' Mum said, still in the same flat voice. 'They're putting in the child protection team. They're going to do an investigation.'

Hot tears spurted out of my eyes.

'I won't go, Mum. I won't let them take me. I'm staying with you whatever.'

'It's all right, love, I know.' This was worse than anger. She sounded defeated, as if her guts had been ripped out. 'They're going after Steve.'

'Good. About time too.' Mrs Judd's mouth snapped tight to stop a smile spreading across her face.

'He's never going to forgive me.' Mum was twisting her hands together.

It was Mrs Judd's eyebrows that snapped together now.

'Marie? I don't believe I'm hearing this. You're not regretting leaving him, are you?'

'He loves me,' Mum said. 'I know he does. And we had some good times, didn't we, Jake? We had some laughs?'

I didn't look at her. I couldn't.

'Anyway, he'll kill me for this,' Mum said.

'No, he won't.' Mrs Judd was taking charge again. 'He'll be too scared. I've known Steven Barlow since I caught him stoning my cat when he was ten. Red-handed. When he saw me he ran as if Dracula was on his tail. He's a coward, is Steven. He's scared of anyone in authority. He only picks on people who can't fight back. Mention a policeman to him and you won't see him for dust.'

I remembered what had happened the day before, when Steve had seen Mrs McLeish and Mr Grossmith watching him, and how he'd let go of me at once.

But it's OK for Mrs Judd, I thought. You'd have to be a nutter to go for her. She'd scare off anybody.

'I'm putting the kettle on,' Mrs Judd said, marching back towards her kitchen. 'Look at your faces, the pair of you. You'd have thought the sky had fallen in. This is the best thing that could have happened, in my opinion. Anyway, it saves me the trouble of reporting Mr Steven Barlow to the authorities myself.'

My head's spinning round these days till I don't know whether I'm coming or going.

89

Everything's changed.

Here's a list: we've left Steve. We've left the flat. We've moved in with Mrs Judd. I told on Steve at school. I've got myself a best mate. My unreal dad has gone off into nowhere in his scarlet uniform. My real dad is . . . I can't get my head round him at all.

I feel different too. I never used to get angry, but I do now. I never used to think I could stand up to anyone, but sometimes I think I can now.

I reckon there's some of Mrs Judd in me. She's my grandma, after all.

We've got a real fight on our hands now, Mrs Judd and me. We're in it together and it's going on all the time. It's her and me against Mum. Since the day the school phoned up and told her they were going to go after Steve, Mum's been on and on about him.

'Say what you like, he's not all bad,' she says. 'He's looked after us all these years.'

'Looked after!' snorts Mrs Judd, and I raise my eyebrows too. 'He damn nearly killed your son, Marie. He terrorized you.'

Mum won't look Mrs Judd in the eye.

'I'm not saying we didn't have our bad times,' she says, going all obstinate on us. 'But there were good times too.'

'Like when?' I chip in. 'Like when you got me that space station at Christmas and he trashed it on Boxing Day? Like when he was trying to belt me and you got in between us and he landed one on you and broke your collar bone?'

She looks shifty.

'It was accidental. He didn't mean it.'

'No. He meant to break mine,' I say, and I feel my

new anger flare up. It's a hard feeling, a shiny kind of feeling, and it makes me feel good.

'If you go back to him, Mum,' I say, 'I won't go with you. I won't. I'll stay here with Grandma, or I'll run away.'

Then I see her wavering, and it's so awful I can't bear to watch. I see my mum trying to choose between the meanest man in the universe, and me, her son.

'Go on, then,' I say, and I'm petrified my anger is going to go and I'm going to start crying. 'Go back to him. You know what he'll do, don't you? He'll start on the baby. The minute she cries, he'll go for her.'

She gives me a funny look.

'Why do you keep saying 'she'? How do you know it's a girl?'

'I just do.' I don't want her to be distracted. 'So who's it going to be, Mum? Steve or me?'

So far, things have always ended the same way, with her saying, 'Give over, Jake. What you take me for? I'm your mum, aren't I?' But I'm not too hopeful. If he turns up here in his best shirt, stinking of aftershave, with a bunch of flowers in his hand, I think I know what'll happen. He'll be all smarmy, and she'll go all gooey, and he'll make promises, and she'll say she believes them, and that'll be that. We'll be out of here and home again before you can say 'lying bastard'. It'll be back to the old terror, night and day.

I keep reckoning without Mrs Judd, though. She's a fixture in our lives now. She in there with us, and she's rooting for me.

He did come round with flowers, like I was afraid he would, only thank God he got his timing wrong. Mum had got back from work so tired she looked like death, and Mrs Judd had sent her upstairs to have a bath.

'Do you good,' she said. 'Relax yourself. There's some bubble stuff on the shelf. Don't worry about supper. It'll keep.'

Mum had rolled her eyes at me when Mrs Judd had marched back into the kitchen. Mrs Judd was bringing out all kinds of new things in Mum. Sometimes it was great, and they were laughing and gossiping and joking like a couple of sisters, and sometimes Mum was like a little girl, lapping up all this spoiling one minute, then going rebellious and naughty the next.

'Relax in a hot bath,' she'd mouthed at me as she went up the stairs, making a funny face. 'Supper will be served in half an hour.'

I'd giggled and gone back to the telly in the living room. One of the nicest things about being at Mrs Judd's, was having a say in what we watched on TV. At the flat, it was always what Steve wanted, and if I sat in the big armchair when he was out, and he came back and caught me in it, he'd kick me off it, whether he wanted to sit down himself or not.

I heard the water run upstairs, and then the doorbell rang. I didn't want to answer it myself, but I didn't have to. Mrs Judd was opening the door almost before I was out of the sitting room.

I could smell his aftershave before I even saw him. It made me want to puke.

'It's all right, Mrs Judd,' he said at once, in a

wheedling voice, smiling till I thought his cheeks would crack. 'I've come to apologize for my hasty words the other night. All I want is to sit down and talk things over with Marie.'

'Oh, do you?' said Mrs Judd. 'Really.'

'Is she all right?' said Steve. 'I've been that worried about her, with her being pregnant and all.'

'Get lost, Steven.' Mrs Judd started to shut the door.

His smile slipped.

'I've got my rights,' he said, his voice hardening. 'Let me in.'

'It wouldn't do you any good if I did,' she said. 'She's out.'

'Out?' His eyebrows nearly met across the top of his nose in a thunderous frown. 'Where? Who with?'

'She's talking things over with her social worker,' said Mrs Judd triumphantly.

I was getting worried. Mum had the taps running, but if she turned them off, and Steve heard, he'd realize she was there, and nothing would stop him barging past Mrs Judd and up the stairs. And if she heard his voice she'd have a towel wrapped around her and be down in a flash, batting her eyelashes and dabbing at her hair.

Then, thank God, I heard music wafting down the stairs. She'd taken the radio into the bathroom with her. With any luck she wouldn't hear a thing.

Anyway, Mrs Judd had got it right. The words social worker had got to Steve. He was too rattled to notice the noise from upstairs. I could see the change come over his face, the anger redden his eyes. He was

93

losing it. I backed away into the sitting room and watched through the crack of the door.

'Old bag!' he snarled. 'Interfering cow!'

'Have they been on to you yet, Steven?' Mrs Judd said sweetly. 'They will soon, if they haven't already. They're calling a case conference about the violence that's been done to Jake. Didn't you know? The meeting's on Thursday. Social workers, teachers, lawyers – oh, they'll all be there. The police too, of course.'

I could see by Steve's face that he knew about the case conference.

He muttered something.

'What was that?' Mrs Judd said. 'I don't think I heard. They're going to decide about taking legal proceedings against you. So here's a piece of free advice. You're in deep trouble already, and if you don't want worse, stay away from Jake and Marie. Next time I see your face round here I'm calling the police.'

Steve seemed to recover a bit.

'That's what you said last time, but you didn't, did you?'

'Oh get lost, Steven,' Mrs Judd said, as if she was losing patience with an irritating little boy.

Steve seemed to turn into one, before my eyes. Then he went back to being smarmy again.

'Just give her these,' he said, and he pushed the flowers into her hands and turned round, and I saw him wriggling his shoulders under his leather jacket as he went out of the gate, as if he'd won some kind of victory.

Upstairs, the radio had stopped and I could hear Mum moving about.

'Quick, Jake, put these in the bin,' Mrs Judd said, shoving the flowers into my hands.

I waited a moment or two, getting my courage up, then I went to the front door and looked up and down the road. I could see Steve walking away, and feeling safe I took the flowers to the dustbin by the gate and rammed them down, head first, on top of a heap of manky chicken bones, till all the stems were snapped. I stirred the whole thing up a bit so Mum wouldn't see them if she took the lid off the bin. And then, I don't know why, I spat on it all.

When I got back to the door Mum was coming downstairs. She was sniffing the air, with a wistful look in her eyes. 'What's that smell?' she said.

'Air freshener,' I said quickly. 'I had some dog shit on my shoe. Grandma blasted the place to get rid of the stink.'

'Oh,' she said sadly, and drifted off to the kitchen, and I stood there, feeling almost guilty, as if I'd betrayed her, and telling myself off for being a fool.

This is what I was thinking when I went to bed in my dad's old room that night.

I was thinking about fathers. About what they should be like.

A father should be fit, strong enough to go after anyone who threatens his kids. He shouldn't have enemies, though. He would be friends with people outside his family, so that his son would feel good walking down the street with him. People would come up to them and say, 'Is this your son? Nice kid.'

His son wouldn't have to be quiet all the time, and slip past people trying not to be noticed, with shameful bruises on him, and dirty secrets in his head. He'd hold himself up straight, and call out to his mates, if he saw them in the distance, and laugh out loud, even out of doors, whenever he liked.

A father ought to let his kids be at ease in their house, not make them want to freeze, or run away and hide when he comes in. He wouldn't trash their stuff or swear at them.

He'd want to be with them, like reading them stories when they were little, and taking them out to play football, and going places together when they were older. Fishing, maybe, or down to the coast for the day. The funfair and stuff like that.

And if there was a parents' evening at the school, he'd go to it, and his son would be proud of him.

'Is that your dad?' his mates would say, and there'd be respect in their eyes.

His son would never be scared of his dad, not even when he'd been down the pub.

A father shouldn't punch his kid. Or kick him. Or burn him. Or shake him. Not ever, ever, ever.

Sometimes he'd say, 'Good for you, son. You're a good lad. Come here, and give your old man a hug.'

Things aren't ever the way you think they're going to be, not even the biggest moments in your life. Especially not the biggest moments in your life.

It was the biggest moment in my life today.

Mum and Mrs Judd went off to the case conference this afternoon. They'd been fussing about it for days. Mum had had her roots done, and Mrs Judd had had her hair permed, and she was wearing her best coat and shoes.

They were still out when I got in from school. Mrs Judd had shown me where to find the key (under a flower pot on the windowsill), so I could let myself in.

I hadn't been in the house on my own before. It felt weird. I half wanted to go round and look at everything, poke around in Mrs Judd's bedroom, and in drawers and cupboards. But it didn't feel right so I didn't.

Instead I got myself a cup of tea and a couple of chocolate biscuits out of the tin on the side, and did the usual. Lay down on the sofa in front of the TV.

When I heard the key in the front door I thought it was them coming home, and I sat up and brushed the crumbs off my sweatshirt and tidied up the cushions a bit.

It wasn't them, though. No, it wasn't them.

There was a kind of pause in the hall, and I heard a heavy bag being put down on the floor. I must have been waiting for this moment without realizing it, because I guessed at once who it was.

I felt cold all over. I think I started shaking, but I'm not sure. Whenever I try to remember exactly how it was, my brain turns to jelly.

The sitting room door opened and he came in.

He was a bit shorter than I'd expected, and heavier, but I knew him at once, even though he wasn't at all the way I'd imagined him. Not one bit. He wasn't fat, really. Just well-rounded. He had one little gold earring and his fair hair was very short.

Almost stubble. You could only just see the place in front where it grows straight up.

He was frowning at me.

'Who the hell are you?' he said.

I never thought, in all my life, that those would be the first words he'd say to me.

He must have thought I was goofy, staring at him with my mouth half open, but I could hardly breathe. My head was being squeezed tight.

This isn't happening, I told myself. He's not real.

'How did you get in here? Where's my mother?' He thinks I broke in, I thought, in a panic. He reckons I'm a burglar.

'I'm Jake,' I said. 'I'm . . .'

I couldn't tell him any more. Why? Why couldn't I say, 'Hello, Dad. I'm your son!'

'Jake?' he was staring at me now.

'You're Danny, aren't you?' I said.

He sat down suddenly on the easy chair opposite the sofa, as if his knees had given away.

'What's your other name, Jake? Who's your mum and dad?'

He sounded breathless, and he'd gone a sort of pale colour.

'My mum's Marie.' I couldn't say about my dad, so instead I said, 'Mrs Judd's my grandma.'

He shook his head disbelievingly, but his eyes never left my face.

At last he said, quite quietly. 'You're my son. You're Jake, aren't you? You're really him.'

What did I expect him to do next? Stumble across the room and hug me? Burst into tears? Punch the air and say, 'Yes! To think that I've found you again after searching so long and so far.'?

He didn't do anything like that. He just made a nervous noise in his throat. All the time he was staring at me, staring and staring, his mouth hanging open in amazement. And my whole life was beginning to fall in, and Steve's voice was there in my ear, saying, 'His *son*? Your *dad*? He never gave a toss for you.'

Then I saw a kind of light go on in his eyes, and this big stupid grin came over his face. He dropped his head and put his hand over his eyes, but only for a moment, before he lifted it again. I had the idea that he'd thought I'd be gone when he looked up.

'My God.' He was almost whispering. 'You really are. My baby. Jake.'

When he said 'My baby', Steve's voice went away out of my head, and I knew I was grinning too.

He stood up and came over to sit beside me on the sofa. I could feel him trembling.

'You're just like me, like I was. You've got my hair. Your two front teeth are crooked, like mine.'

'I know. I saw you in the photo in the hall. It's how Grandma knew who I was, because I looked so like you.'

He jumped up, as if he couldn't sit still another moment, while I was frozen to the sofa. Then he turned round and sat down again. And he picked my hand up and looked down at it, and there I was, with my hand in my dad's, and we were so close we were touching each other. We'd both got the shakes so hard now I thought my teeth would start chattering, but it didn't matter. A moment later I felt something pass between us, I don't know what it was.

'Jake,' he said again. 'I can't . . . I don't . . . this is so weird. I never dreamed . . . Why are you here? Where's Marie? Where's my mum, come to think of it?'

'At the case conference, with the police and social workers and everyone. They're deciding about me.'

'The police? You're not in trouble, are you?'

If his hand hadn't still been gripping mine, I'd have worried then. If he got the wrong idea about me, he might give up on me before we'd even started. But his fingers were holding mine even tighter, as if he wanted to protect me.

'No,' I said. 'I'm not in trouble. Not like that.'

I think it must have been feeling his hand, so big and strong, and maybe the warmth coming off him as he sat close to me, but my feelings boiled up suddenly out of nowhere, like a fountain being switched on.

'Why didn't you ever come and see us?' I said. 'Why didn't you write to me? I wanted you to. I dreamed about you all the time.' I felt his hand twitch. 'I've still got that duck you gave me when I was born.'

I was crying now, but I didn't care. I just sniffed the tears back up my nose.

He made a kind of groaning noise, then he put his arms round me. He did. He put them round me. I could smell the sweat on him, and soap. Nice smells. The collar of his shirt was against my cheek. His chin was pressing down on the top of my head.

Then I realized he was crying too.

That jerked me out of it. I didn't want him to stop holding me, even though I was getting cramp in my shoulder, but I had to give another gigantic sniff and that made him let me go.

He wiped his face on his cuff.

'Jake,' he said, 'I don't know what to say. I'm all over the place. I'm just . . . This has knocked me out. You've got no idea. All these years I've . . . I don't even know how you got here. Why you're here.'

'I'll tell you, but you tell me first.'

He swallowed and looked down. He let go of my hands and felt around in his trouser pocket. He pulled out a crumpled tissue and blew his nose.

'It's not what you might think. It's not that I didn't care. When Marie told me she was going to have my baby I was over the moon. Delirious. I came to see you in the hospital when you were born. I held you in my arms. At that moment, if anyone had come near you, to hurt you, I'd have ripped the stuffing out of them and sent them off to kingdom come.'

I'd never listened to anyone the way I was listening to him. It was if my heart was in my ears.

'And then . . .' He stopped. 'Well, I don't know how to say this. My mother didn't believe you were my baby. She kept telling me that Marie had been going around with some of the other lads. Do you know what I'm saying, Jake?'

'Yes.'

'I didn't listen to her. Not at first. But she was so certain. She kept on about dates, making out it couldn't have been me because I was away at camp when you – when it must have happened.'

'When she got pregnant.'

101

'Yes.'

'The doctor reckoned I was early, by three weeks or something. That's why I was so small.'

'Marie never knew when you were due or anything. She was vague about it.'

'She was sixteen,' I said. 'Like she says. No one knows anything about anything when they're sixteen.'

He smiled.

'Don't I know it.'

'So it was Grandma who talked you out of thinking you were my dad?'

'I suppose so. Yes.' He looked dead guilty then. 'I didn't want to believe her, but she was that certain. I suppose you'll think I'm a real patsy, thinking what my mum told me to think.'

'Oh, no,' I said. 'Not when your mum's Mrs Judd. I know her. You'd have to be Tarzan or Superman or someone to stand up to her.'

We grinned at each other, as if we were allies.

This is the first thing we've shared, I thought, and my heart was leaping for joy.

He was shaking his head again.

'I'm never going to get over this. I can't . . . I'd never have believed . . .'

He stopped.

'I knew you'd gone off into the army,' I said. 'I used to collect pictures of soldiers. I used to imagine one of them was you, and I'd talk to it.'

He flinched as if I'd hit him, and made a little groaning noise.

'But you didn't quite believe your mum, did you?'

I said quickly, not wanting him to get upset, 'because you wrote that letter.'

'It was because of what I felt when I saw you in the hospital. I was so sure you were my baby. I couldn't get it out of my head. I've never got you out of my head. You were this great big question mark hanging over me. It got bigger, not smaller. I was so scared I'd dumped my own kid. Once I thought I was going to have another baby, but it didn't come to anything.'

'She had an abortion. Grandma told us.'

He looked surprised.

'What's got into Ma? She really has spilled the beans.'

'It's because she feels guilty. She keeps talking about missing out on being a grandma, and saying she never got the chance to take me down the park to feed the ducks. She's cooking all these gigantic meals all the time to make up for it.'

'Take my advice. Don't eat them,' he said, patting his tum. 'Look what she's done for my weight. Anyway, it serves her right. What about me? It was her fault I never got the chance to be a proper dad.'

'But you wrote that letter,' I said, 'like you knew I was your son.'

He bit his lip.

'I know this sounds bad. Don't get me wrong, Jake. I wanted to make sure. Like I said, I couldn't get you out of my head. That letter was sort of a test. When you were born, Marie went on and on about money. Maintenance, you know? Mum said that was all she was after, trying to con me out of my wages. So when I wrote I told myself if she wrote back with stuff about you, and how you were getting on, if she answered all my questions, I'd know I really was your dad, but if she just asked for money – well.'

'And she just went on about the money.'

I didn't know if I ought to be more angry with Mrs Judd for turning my dad against me, or him, for letting her, or Mum, for screwing up her letter.

'We were kids,' he said, as if he was pleading with me. 'Just a couple of silly kids. Not a lot older than you are now.'

I hadn't thought of it like that. There was no point, really, in blaming them. I'd save up my anger for Steve, who deserved it.

There was something I wanted to know, though, before I started telling him about Steve. I had to swallow hard before I asked him.

'Are you pleased to see me?' I said. 'I know it's a bit of a shock, but do you mind?'

He made a funny noise, like a choke or a gasp, deep down in his throat.

'Mind? *Mind*? This is the happiest day of my whole life!'

He leaned forward and hugged me again, really tight, and I hugged him back, and we were sitting there on the sofa, hugging and crying and laughing, when the door opened and Mum and Mrs Judd walked into the room.

I thought there was going to be a massive explosion straight off. A real fireworks display. But to start with all that happened was that Mum flushed up a bit and said, 'Oh, it's you, is it?' and Mrs Judd said, 'Where the hell have you been, Danny? I've been trying and trying to get hold of you,' and my dad jumped up and straightened his jacket and looked awkward, and said, 'Hello, Marie.'

I was sweating with nerves. I barged straight in, because I didn't want them to get started.

'What happened at the case conference?' I said. 'Are they going to take me away?'

'They're taking you nowhere, love,' said Mrs Judd. 'Like I said. Over my dead body.'

'You know what you are, Danny Judd,' said Mum. She'd been standing there, getting steam up, taking no notice of Mrs Judd and me. 'You're a rotten little shyster, and I've waited all these years to tell you to your face.'

'No, he's not, Mum. Don't,' I said. 'He didn't know he was my dad. It wasn't his fault. He thought I was someone else's.'

'He *what*?' Mum's face went redder still, and I saw that I'd put my big foot right in it. 'So that was what you thought, was it? I was a slag, was I?'

'Marie, listen,' said my dad, looking desperate.

'The truth is,' my grandma said heavily, 'that it was all my fault. I persuaded him, Marie. He didn't want to listen to me, but I did my sums and I reckoned it couldn't have been Danny, because he was off at camp. I didn't know till you told me the other day that Jake was premature.'

'Bugger your sums!' shouted Mum. 'That wasn't it! You just couldn't bear the idea of your precious little Danny having it off with a tart like me.'

Mrs Judd looked flustered.

'I know I did wrong, and I'm so sorry for it. You know I am. I'm going to regret it for the rest of my

105

life. But it wasn't only because it was you. I thought he was too young to have sex with anyone.'

'Yeah, but they were sixteen,' I chipped in. 'Loads of people in my year at school have had sex. They say they have, anyway.'

'What?' They all turned and stared at me, and I saw I'd really shocked all three of them.

'That's disgusting,' said Mrs Judd. 'You're only kids.'

'We're not.'

'Jake!' Mum was glaring at me. 'You haven't been . . .'

'Give me a break, Mum.' I was really embarrassed, in front of my dad and everything, but he laughed and put his arm round my shoulders and squeezed them.

'Well, whatever, Marie,' he said. 'You can call me all the names you like. I deserve it. But it's like all my Christmases and birthdays rolled into one to come in here and find Jake. My own son! I'm so proud of him I don't know what to do with myself. I just wish you hadn't had to bring him up on your own.'

The fizz went out of Mum then. She bit her lip and looked away from him.

Steve, I thought. She's got to tell him about Steve. It's got to come out now.

'You two have a lot of catching up to do,' Mrs Judd said, looking from one to the other. 'Come on, Jake. Come into the kitchen and give me a hand with the supper. We'll have to do extra now Danny's come home.'

*

What Mrs Judd means when she tells you to give her a hand in the kitchen is that you sit down at the table, and she whizzes round you and stops you trying to do anything. Except for drying up. She lets me dry up sometimes.

There wasn't any drying up to do, though, so I just sat down and worried about what was going on in the front room.

I thought, if I keep my fingers and feet crossed, and touch as much wood as I can, with my hands and arms and legs, maybe they'll make it up. They must have been in love once, or I wouldn't be here.

'People can fall in love again, a second time round, sort of thing, can't they, Grandma?' I said.

She was stirring something on the cooker and she turned round and looked at me.

'I know what you're thinking. Better not. It won't happen.'

'It could, though. He hasn't got anyone now, has he? And she's split up with Steve.'

She shook her head.

'There's been too much water under the bridge.'

'I suppose you mean his being married once, and Steve, and the baby and everything. I can see the baby might be a problem. Maybe my dad wouldn't like it, her having Steve's baby.'

'It's none of his business. She's not his girlfriend any more.'

'No, but she might be. I mean, it could happen.'

'Don't, love.' She bent forward to taste a spoonful of whatever was bubbling in her saucepan. 'Don't get your hopes up. You'll only end up breaking your heart over it.'

107

She was right to warn me. It can't have been more than another ten minutes before I heard shouting coming from the front room, and my bright little dream smashed like a fallen bubble of glass. Then the kitchen door opened, and my dad stormed in.

I'd thought he wasn't the type to get angry. I'd noticed, straight off, that his face was open and friendly, with laughter lines round his mouth and eyes. It was the first thing I'd checked out. I reckoned he wouldn't be able to look mean and vicious the way Steve did, even if he tried.

Now, though, his eyes were sparkling with rage and his mouth was tight. I found I was gripping the table, and tightening my face automatically, waiting for the blows to fall.

They didn't. He knelt on the floor beside me and held me by the arms. He was gentle, though his face was wild with fury.

'Show me,' he said. 'What did that bastard do to you? Let me see.'

There wasn't that much left to show him, quite honestly. My face was just about normal again, and the bruises on my ribs and back had faded during the last couple of days to a yellowish colour with only a few bits of purple in the middle.

The trouble was, his anger was paralysing me. Terrifying me. I couldn't move.

'It's all right, Jake,' he said, and he put one hand on my shoulder. 'I don't believe this. You're scared stiff, aren't you? You poor kid, you think I'm going to do you over. You think I'm like him.'

I couldn't say anything. I was trying to breathe properly, trying to smile.

'I would never lay a finger on you, never.' He was speaking really quietly, like he was trying to reassure me. 'You're mine. My kid. I'd just as soon hit myself. Anyway, I'm not like that. Beating up kids doesn't turn me on. There's only one person I'd want to lay into. Come on, Jake. Show me.'

He took hold of the bottom of my sweatshirt and started to lift it up. Mum was standing in the door now.

'Danny, I couldn't stop him,' she was saying, crying into a tissue. 'I tried. You don't know what he's like when he gets going.'

My dad was looking at my back. I twisted my head round to look at him. His face was red, and he was biting his lip so hard I thought he'd make it bleed.

'She did try,' I said. 'She couldn't ever stop him. Nobody could. She did her best. Honestly.'

He let go of my sweatshirt and stood up.

'I'm going to kill Steve Barlow for this,' he said. 'He's got no idea what's coming to him. I'm going to tear out his insides and hang them out to dry. He's going to wish he'd never been born.'

If my dad had been Steve, once he'd got angry, that would have been it. He'd have been in a filthy mood for the rest of the evening. No one else would have dared say a word, and I'd have been looking for the first chance to slip off out of it before he got going with his fists.

But my dad made himself calm down. He said, 'I'm not going to let that git spoil the best surprise I've ever had in my whole life. We're going to enjoy ourselves this evening. Steve can wait.'

The three of us, me and my mum and dad, sat down at the table, while Mrs Judd fussed over dishing up the supper. Then my dad jumped up and said, 'Got any of that bubbly left over from New Year, Ma? I feel like celebrating.'

I had another wave of worry, then, in case he was going to get wrecked, and the drink would turn him nasty, but it was OK. We all had some. I'd never had bubbly wine before, and to be honest I didn't like the taste much.

Getting it out turned out to be a good idea, though, because Mum had been really tense and wound up, and it calmed her down a bit, (even the half glass, which was all Mrs Judd let her have) and after a couple of sips Mrs Judd got so mellow she was almost melting into the shepherd's pie she'd fetched out of the oven.

It didn't seem to affect my dad much at all. He just kept staring at me, and grinning, and saying, 'I can't believe this isn't all some amazing dream.'

When Mrs Judd had handed round the pie and the veg, and we were all getting stuck in, she said, 'Don't you want to know what happened at the case conference, Jake?'

'You told me,' I said. 'They're not going to put me in care.'

'Yes, but there's more to it than that. Tell him, Marie.'

'We're going home,' Mum said. She glanced up at Mrs Judd and looked down at her plate again. 'When it suits us.'

I could feel the blood draining out of my face, I sat there with my mouth open, holding my fork halfway up to it, and my stomach was turning over as if I was going to be sick.

'It's OK,' she said, stabbing her fork into a piece of carrot as if she was cross with it. 'Steve's moving out.'

'Who says? He won't go. I don't believe it.'

I felt like someone who's recently come off Death Row after years and years, and has just been told they've got to go back on it again.

'I don't know if I believe it myself,' Mrs Judd said. 'Anyway there's no way you're going back there till we're sure it's safe for you.'

'I'll damn well be the one to make sure you're safe,' my dad said, making a growling noise in his throat.

'Don't be so soft, Danny.' Mrs Judd waved her fork at him. 'You'll be back up the M6 any day now. You won't be here to do anything. The point is, there's a court injunction out on Steve. He'll be arrested if he comes to the flat or goes anywhere near Jake.'

'Oh.'

I looked over at Mum. She was pushing the food round on her plate, and her mouth was pulled down at the corners.

'I could stay here with Grandma,' I said. 'Then Steve could go on being with you, if you want, Mum.'

I don't know why I kept messing things up, but I'd done it for the millionth time. Mum looked as if she was going to start off crying all over again.

'Oh, thank you very much. First my boyfriend

111

pushes off, then my own son says he doesn't want to live with me any more.'

'No!' I was stuck. I didn't know how to get out of it. 'Of course I'd rather be with you than—' I stopped. I was scared now that if I said too much I'd end up offending Grandma too. 'I just thought, if you'd rather be with Steve, and you couldn't, because of me, I wouldn't want to be the one to make you unhappy.'

She was twisting a tissue round in her fingers.

'I want to be with you, Mum,' I went on, feeling really anxious now. 'I mean, you're my mum. I want to stay with you whatever. Except not with him. I can't stay with him. And you shouldn't either, not even on your own. If you do, I'll be scared all the time, because if I'm not there he'll go for you. You know he will. And then he'll start on the baby.'

I was trying to work out my thoughts in my head, doing it out loud.

'Anyway, I really want to be there with the baby. She'll need to have a big brother around the place. I'll help look after her. Make sure no one hurts her.'

I reckoned I'd put things right, thank God. Mum did cry a bit, but in a nice way, and Grandma said, 'You're a good boy, darling.'

It was the first time she'd called me darling, and it rattled me a bit, then I reckoned it was because of the bubbly, and that made it OK.

My dad was staring at Mum with his mouth half open.

'You don't mean you want to go back to that bastard, after what he's done to Jake?'

Mum's mood changed again in a flash.

'Oh, it's all right for you, Mr High and Mighty. Steve was there for me, he was, when no one else gave a monkey's. How else could I have managed? He kept a roof over our heads, which is more than anyone here present bothered about, thank you very much.'

My dad shook his head.

'All right, Marie. No need to rub it in. You won't be without support again, financial or otherwise. I've promised you that already.'

'And you won't get rid of me that easily, either,' said Grandma.

No one said anything for a moment. Then my dad rapped his knife on the table.

'Hey, listen to us! We weren't going to let him spoil our evening, remember, and here we've been, talking about him non-stop. Who wants more bubbly? Not you, Jake. Underage sex is one thing, but underage drinking—'

Everyone laughed, except me.

'Dad!' I said. 'I never—'

'What?' He looked startled. 'You called me "Dad".'

I felt nervous.

'Don't you want me to? I won't, then. I'll call you Danny if you like.'

'Don't you dare. You'll call me Dad. It'll take a bit of getting used to, that's all, but I'm going to love it. You can shout it down the street at the top of your voice and watch my chest stick right out of my shirt with pride.'

*

113

I thought Dad would want his room back. I went upstairs and started bundling up all my stuff, but I'd hardly got started when he walked in.

'What are you doing?' he said.

'All my mess. I'll get it out of your way.'

'Don't be daft. This is your room now. I'm sleeping on the sofa downstairs.'

He sat down on the bed and picked up the red water pistol that was lying on the floor.

'This is brilliant.'

'Grandma gave it to me. I'm too old for it really.'

'Yeah, but it's great. I always wanted one of these. She wouldn't ever buy me one.'

We caught each other's eye and laughed.

'She spoils me rotten,' I said.

'Lie back and enjoy it. Wait till I get started.'

His eyes were wandering round the room. Fluffy duck was on my pillow, but he didn't see it. I was quite glad. That old toy belonged to the other dad, the unreal one. It made me feel embarrassed, somehow.

'I keep thinking of all the fun things we could do next time I'm home,' he said. 'Fancy going to a football match? How about the zoo?'

I looked away from him.

'Not the zoo.'

'I know what you mean,' he said comfortably. 'I don't like seeing animals caged up either. It's cruel. Know what I'd really like? To win the lottery and go on one of those safaris to Africa. To see lions and elephants and stuff in the wild. Just you and me. Holiday of a lifetime. How about it?'

'Oh, wow. Oh, yes!'

A vision came into my head, of my island, and the chimps and gorillas, and the gold and silver apples, and for a moment they were all real, just out there beyond the walls of my dad's bedroom.

'OK, then. You're on.'

'What about Mum? Would she come too?'

He laughed.

'Marie? In Africa? You know what she's like with creepy crawlies.'

'Yes, but—'

'No, son. This dream's for you and me.'

'We couldn't really do it though, could we, Dad?'

'One day, maybe. Like I said, if we win the lottery. Or I work my socks off and save up all my cash. Why not? We can dream.'

When he went he left the door open. I didn't shut it. I wanted to go on hearing the sound of his voice from downstairs and the occasional burst of laughter.

I got into my pyjamas and climbed into bed. It was earlier than usual, but I was so tired suddenly I couldn't have stayed up a moment longer.

My eyes were shutting and I was drifting away when I heard his voice clearly from the bottom of the stairs.

'Come on, Marie. You've got to tell me. I'm not going to do anything daft, but I've got to sort this out. Where can I find him? Where does he go when he wants a drink?'

She murmured something I couldn't hear.

'Give over, girl. Have I got a sawn-off shotgun? Where's my rocket launcher? Do I look like a murderer?'

She spoke more sharply this time.

'It's not you, it's him. He goes out tooled up in the evening. Knives.'

I sat bolt upright. My heart started banging inside my chest.

Dad whistled.

'Nice company you've been keeping. You need your head examining, Marie. OK. Sorry I spoke. And stop looking so worried. It takes two to bundle. I didn't mean what I said about hanging his insides out and all that stuff. I'm not into violence, you know that. I just want to keep that slimy bastard off my kid.'

I didn't hear what she said next, or what he answered, but then I heard her say, 'Down the Coach and Horses, usually. But mind your back, Danny, that's all.'

He shut the front door quietly after him, but the sound of the lock catching went right through me. I nearly jumped out of bed and ran to the window to call him back, but I didn't. Then I thought I'd get dressed and sneak out of the house and run after him. I'd even swung my legs out of bed, when I heard a car door slam and the engine start up. I hadn't thought that he might have a car out there. He'd have time to go ten rounds with Steve, or to be murdered twenty times over, before I even got within sight of the Coach and Horses.

I lay there fretting in bed, with awful pictures running through my head, seeing Steve lunge at Dad with a knife, and Dad lying on the floor in a pool of blood, and ambulances racing to the hospital, and doctors crowding round him, then lifting their heads and shaking them at each other.

All the wonders of the day fizzed up inside me and bubbled away to nothing, and I sobbed, and turned on my face with my fists grinding into the pillow.

It was the worst thing, worse even than not knowing him at all, to meet him, and start to love him, and have him taken away, destroyed, like everything else, by Steve.

I was swimming around in sea of misery, thinking about his funeral, and what Grandma would do, when I heard the car stop outside the house, and the door slam. There were footsteps on the path, and the sound of the key in the lock.

I lay and listened with every nerve tingling. Then I heard a burst of film music from the telly as the sitting room door opened.

'What did you want to go after him for, at this time of night?' Grandma's voice was rough with disapproval. 'He's more dangerous when he's tanked up. You've got to watch your step, Danny. You've got responsibilities now.'

'Stay out of it, Ma.' I hardly heard Dad's words. Just the sound of his voice was turning my blood to liquid gold. 'He wasn't there, anyway. The barman told me he's not been around much these last few weeks. Is Jake asleep?'

'Out like a light hours ago.'

'He's a smashing kid, Ma.'

'I know. I'm sorry, Danny. I did it for the best.'

There was silence and I thought they'd both gone into the front room. Then Dad said, 'I know you did, Ma. I just wish—'

And Grandma said, 'Yes. Me too.'

\*

**117**

It's Saturday today.

Dad phoned up his boss this morning and said he needed time off for urgent family business. I was sitting on the bottom step of the stairs while he was talking and he turned and winked at me.

'What's the urgent family business?' I said, when he'd put the phone down.

'Taking you down the shops for starters. Thought you might like some of those upmarket rollerblades.'

I ought to have been really excited, but it worried me, the thought of him spending lots of money. For one thing I knew Mum wouldn't like it. It would set her off again about maintenance and child support and stuff. And the other thing was I didn't trust presents. People give them to you sometimes, and as soon as you like them and start using them they snatch them back, and go on about how grateful you ought to be.

'What's the matter?' he said, watching me. 'Don't you want rollerblades?'

'There'll be loads of people in the shops,' I said. 'It's Saturday. Could we just go to the park and play football?'

'Yes! Whatever you want.' He flexed his biceps. I reckon I can still give you a runaround. I used to be dead fit when I was in the army. Going to seed now. You'll be keeping me on my toes, I can tell.'

Grandma fussed when she heard we were going out, wanting us to take coats in case it rained.

'Yes, yes,' Dad said, brushing her off, and pushing me out of the door.

That gave me the giggles and once I'd started I couldn't stop, not because of Grandma and Dad, but because of being there, with him, out in the street, alive, together, going somewhere, happy.

We didn't bother with the bus. We walked into town. It was the same way I'd walked every day on my way to school since I'd been at Mrs Judd's, but it was quite, quite different. The leaves in people's front gardens were a brighter green. The slit in the letter box on the street corner was a smile. The cars in the main road weren't growling. They were humming.

The park was on the other side of the town centre. We had to go past the post office, cross the pedestrian lights, turn up towards the supermarket, then cut through the back alley behind the Odeon.

This is where Dad and Mum used to meet, I thought, looking up at the high brick walls, covered with graffiti, and the old film posters peeling off the bricks. And Steve and all their gang were here too.

I looked sideways at Dad, but he was jiggling the football around in his hands and I could see he wasn't thinking about any of that.

Why don't you ever get premonitions when you really need them? I get them all the time, but they're totally useless. I get scared for no reason at all, thinking something's just about to happen, and it never does. But this time, when I could have done with a bit of warning, when we ought to have been on our toes, senses prickling, eyes alert, we went blindly into it before we had a clue.

It happened in a flash. One minute a window cleaner was there in front of us in the narrow alleyway, putting his bucket of soapy water down by the wall, and whistling to himself as he went off round the corner to fetch his ladder, and there was

119

no one around, except for a cat, crouching down beside the bucket and watching it, as if he expected a mouse to jump out of it. And the next minute there was Steve, coming right towards us, his eyes on the ground and his shoulders hunched down.

Dad came to a halt and stood square across the alley. He put out an arm to stop me going on, but he didn't need to. My legs wouldn't have moved if I'd tried to make them. All the blood seemed to have drained out of my head and I thought I was going to pass out.

Steve didn't look up till the last moment, till he was almost bumping into us. Then he lifted his head, and moved one shoulder angrily forward, before he even recognized us, like he always did if he felt someone was in his way.

Then he saw it was Dad and me.

For a moment he looked dead scared. Then he stepped back and fixed a little smile to his mouth.

'Well, well,' he said. 'Look who's here. Long time no see.'

I was a little bit behind Dad, but I was watching out. I had my eyes on Steve's hands. My brain was working double time now, even if my legs weren't up to much. Steve didn't carry a knife in the daytime, not usually, but just in case he'd got one on him I was working out how I'd jump forward, if he whipped it out, and knock it out of his hand.

Dad didn't say anything, but I could feel his anger, real as heat. He was shaking with it.

'You,' he said.

Steve switched the expression on his face, trying to

120

make himself look surprised and hurt. He's a lousy actor, Steve. Anyone could have seen through that.

'What?' he said. 'What are you looking at me like that for?'

'You've been at my kid,' said Dad. 'He's got bruises worse than a torture victim. All over him. Scum, that's what you are.'

'Watch it.' Steve's eyes were narrowing to slits. 'Who are you, calling me scum? You owe me, Danny. I've paid out for years for this kid of yours. Nappies for his shitty little arse, pizza by the bucketful, wear and tear on the furniture. On and on. You wouldn't know. You ran off and left it all to me.'

'Want me to pay you back?' Dad's shoulders were bunched tight. 'I'll pay you. I'll pay you for every mark and every bruise you've ever left on him.'

Steve shook his head, pretending not to understand. I could see he was trying to turn things round, to look mild and reasonable. He'd put his hands in his pockets, and his head on one side. I knew him like that. I knew his voice in this mood. It meant danger. It made my blood freeze.

'I don't get it,' he was saying. 'Marie, and Jake here, and me, one day we're just an ordinary family, with our ups and downs I grant you, and the next day everyone's on my back. Little Saint Jake gets himself done over in a fight at school, and whose fault is it? Mine. He tells a bunch of porkies about me and everyone believes him.'

He sounded so innocent I was scared for one horrible moment that Dad would fall for it, that they'd turn on me together, and the old nightmare would be on me again, but then he looked at me, Steve did, and

121

he lost it, and his mask dropped, and hatred, pure and simple, sparked out of his eyes.

'You lying little—' he said.

He didn't get any further. Dad's fists shot up. Everything around us seemed to go strangely still. I stopped hearing the cars and buses in the street at the end of the alley. There was no noise now except for their breath coming quickly and the scrape of Steve's foot on the paving slabs underfoot as he shifted himself sideways, braced and ready. The narrow alley seemed like a canyon, miles from anywhere. The shafts of light slicing down through the air seemed to come from a foreign sun.

Dad didn't move, and I was afraid he'd wait too long, let Steve attack him first, and get the advantage. The seconds stretched on for ever.

I didn't see who went in first. I think it was Dad, but Steve lashed back so fast I couldn't tell what had happened. Then I felt the worse kind of jolt in my head and stomach as Steve's fist caught Dad on the side of the head, and Dad staggered back and crashed against the wall.

'Pay me back? Like this? Come on, why don't you?' panted Steve.

I knew that voice, that crowing, mocking, tight snarl of a voice. Steve thought Dad was easy meat. A pushover. He'd go for him now, kicking and punching, till Dad was as good as dead.

And I was useless. All I could do was stand there and watch, frozen by the violence boiling out of Steve.

Dad was still propped up against the wall, half knocked out, trying to get himself together. Steve

122

pulled his foot back, ready for one of his specials, the kick to the knee as vicious as a stab that would bring Dad down to the ground, where he'd be helpless, at Steve's mercy.

I shut my eyes. I couldn't look. Then I heard a surprised grunt and my eyes flew open.

Dad had grabbed Steve's lifted foot, and he was forcing it up, using it like a lever to tip Steve over. He must have moved like greased lightning. He must have judged it just right.

Steve was hopping around on one leg, squealing at Dad to stop, while Dad held the other. Then, with one flick of his hands, Dad tossed him over as easily as if he had been a chunk of wood, and it wasn't my dad who was lying on the ground, it was Steve, at our feet, whining and holding his bum, and saying his spine was cracked.

There was a murderous look in Dad's eyes, and for a moment I thought he was going to go in and kill him. Kick him to death. And I wanted him to. I felt my blood boiling up, and everything went red in front of my eyes. I wanted to run in and kick and stamp and punch.

I couldn't have done it, though. I couldn't have brought myself to touch him, not even with the toe of my shoe. I didn't want to dirty myself.

Dad backed off too, as if he was moving away from a bad smell.

'I always knew you were a mean bastard,' he said, his voice filled with acid. 'I knew it even when we were kids, going round together.' He put his arm round my shoulders, and I could hear how fast he was breathing, and smell the angry sweat on him.

'If you ever go near Jake again,' he went on, 'within five miles, you're going to fetch up in prison. Or hospital. Or both. Come on, Jake.'

The stillness had gone suddenly. The alley was an alley, not a canyon, and the sun was the same old sun as usual. I could hear the traffic round the front of the Odeon again, and people calling out in the street, and girls' voices coming our way. They weren't in sight yet, but I looked towards the sound, and there, right there by the wall, was the bucket of water that the window cleaner had left.

I don't know what made me do it. I didn't have time to think. I just ran over, and picked it up. And then I chucked the water up into the air so that it streamed out in a beautiful silvery arc and landed full on him, right on Steve, drenching his head, plastering his hair down over his face, running in dirty streams down his cheeks, soaking his jacket and his trousers, dripping off his hands and feet.

He spluttered and began cussing me, but his eyes were on Dad, and he shut up almost at once. He got to his feet and staggered off, not looking back, lurching to one side to avoid a pair of girls who had come round the corner now and were giggling behind their hands at the sight of him.

That first game of football with my dad was the best I'd ever played. It was like I was flying. I was dribbling and shooting and tackling and swerving so brilliantly I could have been out there on the turf playing in the World Cup final. I had Dad puffing around, laughing and swearing and tying his feet in knots.

I knew it was a one-off. I'd never play like that again. He was better than me really. Faster and with loads of technique. It was just that I'd been touched by genius for once in my life.

'Where's Mum?' I asked Grandma when we got home.

She jerked her chin up towards the ceiling.

'Up in her room. In the dumps. Go and cheer her up, Jake. Wait, just look at you. Soaked in sweat. Get that shirt off before you catch a chill.'

Mum was lying on her bed with a tissue in her hand. Her top was rumpled up and I could see that the baby was beginning to push her stomach out. It was embarrassing, really, so I didn't look.

'What's the matter, Mum?' I said.

'Oh. It's you.' She gave a gigantic sniff. 'Been out enjoying yourself, have you?'

'Yes.' Something told me I'd better not tell her about the fight with Steve, and the brilliant game of football. 'Do you want a cup of tea or something?'

'No. Don't get her up here fussing around me either.'

'Did you have words with her or something?'

'Words? She had words. I couldn't get a word in edgeways. She's like the Niagara Flaming Falls. She swamps me, Jake. I can't be doing with it any more. I want to go home.'

I swallowed.

'Yeah, but what about—'

'I told you. There's a court injunction out on him. He's not allowed near you. Or me. Not even allowed to be with his own baby.'

She made a hiccuping noise.

'He's still there, though, isn't he? In the flat.'

'He's left. I went round to – just to get a few things this afternoon when old Mrs Misery thought I was going off to Mothercare. He's cleared all his stuff out. Left the place like a pig sty too.'

'Where is he, then?'

'How the hell should I know?'

'But he's got his key still, hasn't he, Mum? He can get back in whenever he likes.'

She turned her back on me so she was facing the wall.

'Hop it, Jake. I've had enough. My head's splitting.'

I tiptoed down the stairs. Grandma was coming out of the kitchen with a tray loaded up with a teapot, a mug, and a stack of biscuits.

'Out of the way, love,' she said. 'I'm just taking this tea up to her.'

'She doesn't want any,' I said quickly. 'I asked. She said not to disturb her because she's going to sleep. I think she's dropped off already.'

'Oh.'

Grandma looked disappointed. She went back into the kitchen. I went after her. Dad was at the table reading the paper.

'She wants to go home,' I said.

'I know,' Grandma said. 'She told me. We had a bit of a barney about it.'

Dad chipped in unexpectedly.

'I don't blame her,' he said. 'She wants to get on with her life. You'll have to go back to the flat some-time, the two of you.'

I felt as if I'd been standing on a platform and one

126

of the planks had been knocked out from under my feet.

Dad must have seen the look on my face.

'It's OK, Jake. Not without safeguards. For one thing, we've got to make sure he's moved out.'

'He has. She went round today to get some stuff. He's taken all his things.'

Grandma rolled her eyes.

'Went to find him, I suppose. I knew she was up to something. The crafty—'

'Stop it, Ma!' Dad sounded quite stern. 'Get off her back. Where's Steve staying, Jake?'

'She doesn't know.'

'I'll find out.' He was tapping a finger on the table while he thought things through. 'Next off, I'm going to change the lock. Get you some new keys so he can't walk in and out whenever he fancies.'

I was starting to feel a bit better. Only a bit, though.

'But what if he – you know – hides around the place and catches me when I go out?'

I didn't want Dad to think I was chicken, but I had to get things straight.

'Who's that mate of yours you were telling me about? Kieran, isn't it? Doesn't he live near you? What if you go to school and come home together?'

I thought about that for a minute. I wasn't sure if I knew Kieran well enough yet. Then I remembered how he'd come to my rescue when Mr Grossmith was giving me the going over in the library.

I nodded.

'We could do that.'

'I don't think we'll have to worry for long,'

Grandma said. 'Steve'll be mad as hell for a bit, then he'll get used to things. Like I keep saying, he's chicken, Steve is. Always has been. He picked on Jake because he was a kid, but the whistle's been blown on him now. He'll be running scared.'

I remembered Steve walking off round the corner by the Odeon, beaten and dripping wet, like a dog who's been whipped and crawled out of a puddle.

Maybe they're right, I thought. Maybe it will be OK.

But in my heart of hearts I was afraid.

In my mind, the flat's always been a dark place. There were red-hot danger zones in it, like Steve's chair in front of the telly, and the video shelf, and his side of the bedroom he shared with Mum. If I dared set foot in them, when he was around, that was it. That was IT.

There were my hiding places too, places where I'd hidden my things, and sometimes hidden myself.

But there was nowhere I'd felt safe. He'd always found me anyway, and when I'd tried to hide, it had only made things worse.

We went back to the flat together, my mum and dad and me. When Mum opened the front door, I could smell it in the air, his smell, his sweat and his aftershave, the smell of fear.

Dad walked from the sitting room into the kitchen and the two bedrooms, clicking his tongue.

'I don't believe it,' he said. 'He's trashed the place. What a loser.'

Mum seemed so depressed by it all, by the shower curtain ripped down, and the bedclothes tossed around on the floor, and the sticky stuff burnt on to the cooker in the kitchen, and the empty space where the telly and video used to be, and her little glass cat that he'd given her once, lying smashed on the floor, that she went straight to her bed and sat down on it, all limp, as if she'd been punched in the head.

I went and looked at my own room. I hardly recognized it to be honest. Steve had turned my cupboard over and everything left in it was lying on the floor. And he'd ripped down my football poster and smashed my alarm clock. There was even a jagged hole in the window where he'd chucked something through it.

It gave me the shivers. I could feel him, as if he was still there, doing it, his anger beating round the room like a huge, mad bird.

Then I felt Dad's arm round my shoulders.

'A clean sweep,' he said cheerfully. 'That's what we need in here. Redecoration. New curtains. I'll put some shelves up for your stuff.'

'What stuff?'

'You'll see.'

It sounded for one beautiful moment as if he was planning to move in with us, but then he said, 'I've got a week left before I go back to work. Should be time enough to get things straight and get you two moved back in. Come on. Let's go down the DIY shop and choose a few colours and bits and pieces. You ever tried painting, Jake? It's fun. You can give me a hand.'

Mum snapped at me when we asked if she wanted to come too, so we went off on our own.

We bumped into nasty old Mrs Fletcher at the

main door of the flats. She's always been mean to us, especially since Mum complained about her cats shitting behind the door downstairs. I keep out of her way if I can.

'What are you doing here, Steve?' she said, in her whiny voice, peering at Dad through her dirty, thick glasses. 'Thought you'd taken yourself off to Bristol.'

'It's not Steve, Mrs Fletcher.' I was really proud of saying it, pleased to show Dad off even to her. 'It's my dad. My own dad.'

'Your what?' She made a kind of mumbling noise, and her chin moved up and down, so that the long black hairs sticking off it waved around like antennae.

'Excuse me.' Dad elbowed past me. 'What was all that about Bristol? Did Steve say he was going there? Did he tell you?'

She stared at him, then she cackled like the wicked fairy in a cartoon.

'Another boyfriend, eh? Well, I never. Quite a goer, that Marie.'

She was horrible. I was pulling at Dad's arm to get him away, but he just went on looking at her, and said, 'Why Bristol? Did he say?'

'Got a job down there, hasn't he? Swore at me when I asked him what it was. Nice manners, I must say. I said did he want me to send the bailiffs after him next time they came to call and he told me to go to hell.'

'When did you see him, then?' Dad was talking really nicely. He didn't charm Mrs Fletcher, though. She looked so suspicious you'd have thought he was a cat poisoner.

'What's all this about? Done a bunk, has he? Thought as much. I never liked him. Had a shifty look in his eye.'

'Bristol,' Dad said, when we'd got rid of Mrs Fletcher and were walking back towards his car. 'Why Bristol?'

'He went there a couple of times,' I said, trying to remember. 'Last year.'

I was feeling great. Bristol was miles and miles away. If Steve had gone to Bristol, I'd be fine. Just fine.

'Yes, but why?'

I frowned, dragging things back into my mind.

'He had a mate there, I think. Someone he met in the pub. This guy went there and set up a garage. Steve said last year we all ought to move to Bristol. Said he was fed up with nosy neighbours. Mum wouldn't go. She likes it round here. Do you think he's gone, Dad? Really gone?'

'Sounds like it. Typical Steve if he has. He was always one to bunk off if there was any sign of trouble. What was all that about the bailiffs? Not in debt, is he?'

'I don't know. It was just Mrs Fletcher going on, I think. She likes stirring it. She always has.'

Where did I get all that stuff from about living by myself at the top of a tower in the middle of an island? We've been working non-stop on the flat this last week, my dad and me, and the better it gets here, the weirder that other place – that dream place – seems.

131

I don't need that place now. Home is good enough for me.

I've never wanted to run home from school before, but I've been living through the school days just waiting to get back. Every day there's been new stuff to see.

Dad got someone in to mend the window in my room. That was the first day. We started sploshing paint around that evening.

I spilled a bit on the floor, but Dad didn't shout at me or anything. He just told me to damn well wipe it up and be more careful in future. Then he spilled some too, and we laughed, both of us together.

When I got back the next afternoon my room was done. It was all blue, like I'd wanted. I can see a few bits we missed but I don't mind them. I think it looks great.

I couldn't believe it, the day after that. He'd put up new curtains, with a black zigzag pattern on them – really cool – and some shelves. The top one wobbles a bit so you can't put heavy stuff up there, but the others are OK. And there was a lampshade too, and a new duvet cover, that nearly goes with the curtains.

He'd chucked out the old table, and there was a nice new one, a bit like a desk, with little drawers in it.

'You can do your homework there,' he said.

I've never bothered much about homework, so I didn't say anything. Anyway, I was too busy looking at the poster he'd stuck up on the wall beside my bed.

It was a big picture of a gorilla, or a chimpanzee. I wasn't sure which.

'You like those big hairy guys, don't you?' he said.

'You said something about them. I thought it would do till we win the lottery.'

I couldn't believe he'd done that. It was as if he'd known, although I'd never told him.

It was the chimp at the zoo that sorted everything out, in a way. If he hadn't peed all over Steve, I wouldn't have laughed, and Steve wouldn't have half killed me, and Mum wouldn't have made her mind up to leave the flat. And we wouldn't have gone to Sunnybrook Road, and got to know Grandma. And I'd never have found my dad.

When I saw that poster, I felt that my dad and me were connected, deep, deep down.

It was Dad's last day today. He's going back to work tomorrow. He's got to go, he says, or he'll get the sack.

He's been getting on Mum's nerves.

'What's this new kettle for?' she was saying when I got home. 'The old one worked all right.'

'The flex was fraying,' said Dad. 'You might have got a shock.'

He kept going to the window and looking out.

'What's got into you?' she said. 'Cat on hot bricks, you are.'

'I'm expecting a delivery.' He was looking guilty.

'Of what? What now?'

'I couldn't resist it, Marie. It was a fantastic bargain. I know you'll like it. I tried it out so I could tell it was really comfortable.'

'What is this? What are you up to, Danny?'

'It's a three-piece suite,' Dad said, looking at me as

if he wanted me to back him up. 'They should be here by now. They said they'd deliver it by five.'

'A what?' Mum's voice was rising. 'What am I supposed to do with a flaming three-piece suite! Where do you think I'm going to put it? Hang it from the ceiling? There's not an inch of space left in this flat.'

'They said they'd take the old chairs away,' Dad said, biting his lip. 'Honestly, Marie. You're going to love it. I know you are. It's really good quality. I mean what's so fantastic about those old chairs? Specially that big wreck in front of the telly. It's got stains all over it and the arms are going through.'

'Are you totally off your head, Danny Judd?' Mum demanded. 'Whose flat is this? What gives you the right? You and your mother! Bossing everyone around! Interfering! I've had enough of the lot of you. You come in here and chuck out my stuff and bring in a load of tat I've never even seen! It's not on, Danny.'

She was trying to work herself up, but I could see she only half meant it. She was excited too, in a way.

'But you've been moaning on about those old chairs for years, Mum,' I said. 'And you never chose them either. Steve got them off the man at the dump. You always said the smell from them turned your stomach.'

It was lucky, really, that the door bell rang then, because there was such a business, getting the old chairs out through the door and down the stairs, and bringing up the new suite, that Mum didn't have the chance to get going again.

And when it was done, and they were all in, there

was nothing she could say. Our sitting room was a different place.

Before there had been Steve's big chair stuck in front of the place where the old telly had been, and the two others had been pushed back against the wall. They'd been a horrible brown grey colour, all covered in dark blobs and shiny, greasy places. But now there was this really comfortable sofa under the window, just asking you to stretch out on it, and a couple of chairs with their arms open, begging you to curl up in them.

They were a light pinky red. And they had cushions to match.

'They'll show the dirt,' Mum said, looking round the room, trying to frown. 'Can you imagine what a baby's going to do to them?'

'You can take the covers off,' Dad said, watching her anxiously. 'They're washable.'

Mum gave up all of a sudden. She sat down on the sofa and even stretched her legs out.

'They're great, Mum, aren't they?'

I was breathing in the lovely fresh smell of them, and just looking round the room, which was new and clean and different. Steve's old chair had kept him in here, holding the shadow of his presence, the ghost of my fear. Now it had gone, and he'd gone too.

Mum let out her breath in a gust. Then she threw her head back and laughed.

'Danny, you're so awful. OK, they're nice. They're lovely. But next time don't spring it on me, all right?'

'Next time?' Dad said, mopping his forehead. 'You think I'm going to buy you a three-piece suite every ten minutes? Think I'm made of money? Give over, girl.'

They actually smiled at each other.

Mum hadn't asked Dad to stay to supper, but he did anyway. He phoned Grandma and told her he wouldn't be back till late and he went out and got a Chinese.

We sat on the new sofa while we ate it and watched the new telly, and Dad and I washed up in the kitchen from the mended tap and put the plates away in the freshly painted cupboard.

'You'll do all right now, Jake,' he said, when we'd finished. 'And I'll be back down again in three weeks for a long weekend.'

I couldn't help shivering then. It wasn't just the fear of what might happen when he wasn't there to protect us any more. It was the thought of being without him again, of losing him, of him slipping away, back into the world he'd lived in before we found each other, back into his life without me.

'Oh, and there's something else.' He went out to where his coat was hanging on the peg behind the front door, pulled something out of the pocket, and put it into my hand. 'A mobile. Keep it with you. I've programmed my number into it. Any time, anywhere you need me, I'll be listening on the other end. If you're in trouble, if you're afraid, I'll be in my car and on my way. Three hours door-to-door it takes me. Day and night. Don't forget.'

There are shadows everywhere. They run round the spaces near our flats and spread down our street. There are dark places by the dustbins and behind the doors, under the stairs and beside the garages, places where someone could lie in wait. And in the lane, between the flats and the railway bridge, there are trees and walls and parked cars. A man could hide in so many places, easily.

I get goose bumps quite a lot. If I see a man in the distance who reminds me of him, or if I hear someone coming up behind me, footsteps in the dark, my blood runs cold and then my heart goes wild, jumping around like a mad kangaroo.

When that happens, what I do is this. I put my hand in my pocket and hold on to my mobile phone. Just feeling it is good. Dad is miles and miles away. He couldn't ever get to me in time, but even if he was only there on the end of the line, just his voice, nothing more, and if someone was trying to get me, it would help. I think it would, anyway.

The worst part was the three or four days after Dad went back up the M6. Kieran had a bug or something, and he was off school, so I had to go and come home on my own.

Until we ran away that night, and started living with Grandma, I hadn't realized what it was like, not being afraid. I'd got used to it at her place, to an open kind of feeling, free, and peaceful and lovely.

Why do I feel scared again, now that Steve's away in Bristol, and there's a court injunction out on him, and my grandma's nearby, like a tigress in the bushes, and I've got my mobile phone? I can't help it, that's why. I can't get over the feeling that he might sneak back and jump out on me, his face set hard as metal and his eyes like ice. And when I'm alone, outside in the street, I remember the window cleaner's bucket, and the soapy water streaking up into the air, and the way it landed full on him and ruined his clothes, and how he looked at me. That's when I shake, and my knees feel weak.

Steve's like a nightmare. You can wake up and tell yourself that he's not there any more, but he is. The fear stays in your head. It comes back to you even when things are fine, in the middle of the day, when you least expect it.

I don't think I'll ever be rid of Steve. I'm afraid he'll be in my head for ever.


Mum was in a panic when I got home. She'd wrenched the door open before I'd had time to turn the key in the lock.

'Where have you been? What the hell have you been up to?'

'Sorry, Mum.' I couldn't understand it. She wasn't like this usually if I was late home from school. Often, she wasn't there herself. 'I was playing football with Kieran.'

I dropped my bag on the floor and tried to hang my jacket up, but it fell off the peg.

'Pick that lot up,' she said, 'and get into your bedroom and sort the mess out. She's coming round.'

'Who? Who's coming round?'

'Mrs Judd. Who do you think? The Queen of Sheba? She phoned up. Said could she come over this afternoon.'

'That's great!' I was pleased. 'She hasn't even seen the flat yet. I want to show her what Dad and me did in my bedroom. We haven't seen her for ages.'

'Ages? We only moved back in here last week.

I knew she'd be round sooner or later. Thought I'd have a bit longer though before she descended.'

'You don't mind, do you, Mum?' I stood by the kitchen door watching her. She was hunting around in the cupboard looking for something. 'I mean, you like her, don't you?'

'Yes! No! You and your questions! I was going to ask her round myself. Later on. She's got me all worked up landing herself on me like this. I'm not ready for it. Where are those perishing biscuits? I had a whole packet of them in here last week. Oh my God. That's it. There's the door. She's here.'

I dived passed her to open it. I couldn't wait to see my grandma, to show her everything. Just to see her again.

She was standing on the step in her brown coat with a big shopping bag in her hand and a curious, half nervous look on her face.

'Hello, Jake, dear,' she said in a bright voice.

She looked back down the stairs before she stepped inside. I could see why. The stairs in our building are disgusting, what with Mrs Fletcher's cats, and the trail of rubbish she leaves every time she takes her bags out to the bins.

Mum had darted into her room, and she came out a few minutes after Grandma had stepped inside with a different jumper on. I could feel she was tense too. She had a don't-pick-a-fight-with-me look on her face.

I can't believe the way Mum's changed since Steve left. She never used to say much before, not even when he wasn't around. But now, especially with Grandma, she'll say whatever comes into her head.

It's as if a bottle's been corked up inside her, and now all the stuff is foaming out of it.

Grandma doesn't seem to mind. She likes a good old barney. She took off her coat and watched me hang it up on the peg, then she followed me into the sitting room, picking her feet up and hanging on to her bag.

When she got in through the door and looked round at everything, at the new suite and the plants Mum keeps on the windowsill, the little dog vase that Steve hadn't smashed, and the net curtains tied back with bows, I could see she was really, really surprised.

'It's very nice,' she said. 'You keep everything nice, Marie.'

Mum fired up at once.

'What did you expect? Rats in the kitchen? Fleas in the carpet?'

Grandma looked flustered.

'Of course not. Here, I've got something for you. A house-warming present as you might say.'

Mum calmed down at once. She's always like that with presents. Really excited. Like me at Christmas when I was five, before I knew any better.

Grandma fumbled in her bag and brought out a box in a plastic bag. She was about to hand it over to Mum when some other stuff fell out too, a bottle of Flash and a scrubbing brush. She bent down quickly and scooped them back into her bag again.

'What are those for, Grandma?' I nearly said. 'Are you going off cleaning somewhere?' but my guardian angel told me to keep my trap shut, because I'd seen Grandma's face, and I'd twigged. She'd come all ready to clean up our flat. She'd thought the place would be a dirty dump and she was planning to give it a going-over.

She caught my eye and I saw that she'd gone red. She'd nearly put her foot in it so badly it would have stuck in the mud for ever. She knew it too.

Luckily, Mum didn't see a thing. She'd taken the plastic bag out of Grandma's hands, pulled the box open and was taking the lid off.

'Oh!' she gasped. 'It's lovely!'

She took it out carefully and put it on her knee. I could see it was the sort of thing she liked, a pretty, decoration kind of thing. It was a little statue, made of white china, of a woman with a baby in her arms.

'It's lovely,' she said again.

Grandma looked pleased and relieved and satisfied all at once.

'Thought it would get you in the mood,' she said, 'for the baby and that.'

'Yes. Well.' Mum put the statue carefully down on the sofa beside her. 'I'm trying not to think about it, to be honest. Got enough on my plate. It's not that easy managing on your own.'

Grandma actually leaned over and patted her hand.

'You'll find someone else some day,' she said. 'Pretty girl like you.'

'With my luck?' Mum sighed. 'Anyway, I'm not much of a picker, as it turns out, am I?'

I was afraid Grandma mightn't like that. I was afraid she'd think Mum was being rude about Dad, so I said, 'Shall I put the kettle on?'

Grandma started getting to her feet.

'Let me.'

'No!' said Mum, flapping her hands, and frowning. 'You're supposed to be the visitor. This is my place, remember? You sit there and take the weight off your feet.'

That was a bit close, I thought, because Grandma's no fairy, but Mum didn't mean to be rude. She was just getting her own back, I could see, for all the times she'd been bossed around in Grandma's kitchen.

I got on with it. I made the tea and set up the tray and took it into them. Grandma was dead impressed, I could tell.

'Clever little cook, isn't he?' she said.

'It's only a cup of tea, Grandma,' I said. 'Have a biscuit.'

Mum gave me a funny look. I knew she was wondering where I'd managed to find the packet. I wasn't going to tell her right out loud that I'd fished it out from the back of the cupboard, under a load of old cartons. Grandma liked them anyway. She had three.

'Have you heard from Danny at all?' she said, brushing crumbs off her skirt. 'I only ask because he hasn't given me a ring this week.'

She sounded almost as if she was going to be jealous.

'Well,' I said, talking cautiously in case she got upset. 'He phoned me on my mobile a couple of times, but probably he was just trying it out to see if it worked.'

'He called me up Thursday, to check if the maintenance had arrived,' Mum said. 'He's being good about money, I'll say that for him.'

'He can afford it.' Grandma took another sip of tea. 'They earn a packet on those long overtime jobs. Better spending it on you than on wine, women and song.'

'Song?' Mum shook her head. 'Danny? He can't sing a note. Didn't you ever hear him do "Dancing Queen"? Even the cats ran away.'

I never know where I am with Mum and Grandma. One minute they're on at each other, and the next they're a couple of old buddies. They were both laughing now, leaning back and giving it everything.

Then the phone rang. Mum jumped up and went outside. I listened at first, like I always do, in case it was Steve or Dad, but she said, 'Oh, hello, Denise,' so I stopped bothering.

'Do you want to see my room, Grandma?' I said. 'It's smashing. Dad and I painted it.'

'Yes.' She looked really keen. I knew she'd want a good look around. She's nosy, but I don't mind that. I like it, in her.

Mum was putting the phone down when we went into the hall.

'Who's Denise?' I said.

'One of the girls from work.' Grandma and I said nothing, so she had to go on. 'There's a gang of them going out on Saturday, down to the cinema.'

I pushed past her. I was dying to show Grandma my room. But Grandma was still looking at Mum.

'I hope you're going with them,' she said. 'You'll enjoy it.'

Mum shook her head.

'Why ever not?' Grandma said.

'She never goes out with other people, without—' I stopped. It seemed indecent, somehow, to say Steve's name now.

Grandma understood, though.

'Yes, but you can now, can't you? It'll do you good. Get you out of yourself. Broaden your horizons.' She looked quite relieved to have a bit of bossing to do. 'I'll come and stay with Jake for you. Do him a bit of supper. Would you like that, Jake?'

I had a sudden whiff in my nostrils of Grandma's kitchen, of sizzling onions and roasting chicken, of creamy custard, and tangy fruit pie, and my mouth watered in spite of itself.

'Can my mate Kieran come too?' I said.

'Here, hang on a minute. Who said I was going out anyway?' said Mum.

'Don't, then,' I said. 'Stay in. We could have a bit of a party.'

Some people wouldn't think it was much of a party, just having one friend round and your grandma coming in to do the tea, but it felt like a party to me.

It was the first time I'd ever had a friend come to our flat as long as I could remember. Or a friendly adult, come to think of it. Mum had never asked anyone in while Steve was around. It was like we'd lived in a kind of prison, with us shut in and the rest of the world kept out.

Mum made her mind up in the end to go out with Denise and the others. Then she got in a state about it.

'What do you think?' she said to Grandma, who'd

arrived hours too early. 'This black skirt or the white trousers? They're both too tight now really.'

Grandma pursed her lips.

'You'll catch your death in that short skirt. Haven't you got something warm? There's a nasty wind out there.'

In the end Mum wore the white trousers and a big red top that hid her stomach. She fluffed her hair out and put on sparkly earrings and sprayed herself with perfume.

'You look great,' I said.

She'd dressed herself up sometimes to go out with Steve, but it had always been a worry. Too much make-up and he'd told her she looked like a tart. Not enough, and he'd said she didn't take pride in herself and he'd go out on his own and leave her at home. Usually he hadn't given her the option. He went out on his own anyway.

'Do I look great? Really?'

She turned round, staring at herself over her shoulder in the mirror.

'Very nice,' said Grandma, 'but mind you don't fall over in those stilettos. You won't do the baby any good.'

The baby's going to be a real thing with Grandma, I can tell.

Mum got herself off at last. I could see Grandma was relieved. She was dying to get into the kitchen and start on the cooking.

She'd only just peeled the potatoes when the doorbell rang. I'd been waiting for Kieran so I dashed to get it.

It wasn't Kieran. It was two big men in long black

coats. They pushed me aside and marched right in as if they owned the place. They smelled of violence. It made me feel sick.

Grandma came out of the kitchen with a spoon in her hand.

'Steve Barlow,' one of the men said, sticking his chest out and standing too close to her. 'Where is he?'

Grandma wasn't impressed.

'What's this? A bank raid? You've got it wrong. Try the High Street.'

'Ha ha,' the man said. 'Very funny. We're debt collectors. Mr Barlow's due to settle up.'

'You're out of luck,' said Grandma calmly. 'He's moved. He doesn't live here any more.'

'That's what they all say.'

'He has!' I said. 'He's gone to Bristol.'

'What a pity,' the man said. 'We'll have to take his stuff instead. Come on, Charlie. We haven't got all day.'

They elbowed past us into the sitting room. They made straight for the telly and started unplugging it from the wall.

My hand went into my pocket and I pulled out my mobile.

'I'm calling my dad,' I said.

'You do that, son,' the other man said. 'Tell him to cough up if he doesn't want his stuff taken away.'

Grandma had followed them into the room. The men had picked up the TV now and were holding it between them.

'Put that television down,' Grandma said, pointing her spoon at them. 'It belongs to my son, Corporal Daniel Judd.' She was stabbing her spoon at them as

146

if it was a pointed finger. 'He's a member of the armed forces, is Danny, with a large number of friends who don't like being messed with.'

The men looked at each other again, and without speaking, lowered the TV to the floor.

The phone in my hand crackled and someone spoke at the other end. Before I could lift it to my ear, Grandma said, 'Give it here,' and she took it out of my hand.

'Guess what, Danny,' she said, her eyes on the men. 'We've got a couple of idiots here trying to remove your TV. They're collecting on Steve's debts, so they've been good enough to inform me.'

The phone crackled some more. Grandma nodded and smiled.

'I thought as much. You'll be here in five minutes? With half a dozen of your lads? Good.'

Dad's voice sounded odd. I was trying to hear what he was saying, but I couldn't make anything out.

'Oh, and, Danny,' Grandma went on. 'They've probably got a van outside. Try not to damage it on your way in.'

She clicked the phone off and handed it back to me. I realized my mouth was hanging open with astonishment, and I shut it.

The men were out of the flat already, walking down the stairs, trying not to look as if they were hurrying.

'Come back, you!' Grandma called after them. 'Put this television set back where you found it.'

The only answer was the crash of the main door as it banged shut behind them.

Grandma closed the door of the flat and went back into the kitchen.

'Mystery solved,' she said, looking satisfied. 'Now we know why Steve did a bunk to Bristol.'

'It was the court injunction, Grandma. You said.'

'That wouldn't have been enough to make him run for it. No, Jake. He must be over his ears in debt.'

'He did the horses a lot,' I said. 'He was always getting Mum's wages off her for the betting shop.'

Grandma shook her head.

'Unbelievable. He's even more of a fool than I thought he was. But the main thing is he won't be back here in a hurry. He'll be keeping his head right down with that lot after him.'

'Grandma,' I said, 'you are totally, totally brilliant. You are the most brilliant person I've ever met in my whole life. Except for Dad.'

She put her spoon down and pulled me into a hug that nearly crushed me to bits. I wasn't bargaining for that. I thought my spine would snap.

When she let me go, I was breathless, as if all the air had been squeezed out of me.

'What did Dad say?' I asked.

'Oh,' she said, picking up her spoon again and turning back to the cooker. 'That wasn't Danny. You pressed the wrong number. I didn't know who it was. I didn't ask. I don't know what they thought of my side of the conversation.'

Mum had to go to the hospital today to have a scan. It's half-term, and Kieran was helping out in his uncle's shop, so I went with her.

We passed Kieran's uncle's shop in the bus. I could

see someone that might have been him, carrying boxes through from the back, but I wasn't sure.

'Does your uncle pay you any money when you help him?' I'd asked Kieran, that night when he came round to our place and Grandma had cooked us a slap-up fried chicken with chips and salad on the side.

'No, but he gives me stuff,' Kieran had said, cramming another chunk of chicken into his mouth. 'It was a radio last time. He said he'd give me a watch next. I'll ask if you can help too, if you like.'

He'd forgotten, but I didn't mind. I wanted to go to the hospital with Mum.

'You'll see the baby on the scan,' Grandma told me. 'Its arms and legs and everything.'

When we got off the bus, and walked in through the big double gate, I turned right automatically, going towards the only part I knew, the doors with Accident and Emergency written over them.

'Not that way,' Mum said, not meeting my eye. 'The antenatal is round the side.'

This part of the hospital was nicer. There are only hard plastic chairs in Accident and Emergency and the nurses are all in a hurry, and there are people shouting and getting angry, and asking you questions that you aren't supposed to answer.

But in the antenatal there are padded chairs to sit on while you wait, and a tea machine in the corner.

When Mum went in for her scan they let me go in too.

It's quite dark in here. The doctor sits in front of a screen.

'On the bed, please,' she says to Mum.

Mum's wearing a hospital gown, and the doctor pulls it up so her stomach's bare. It sticks out a good bit now. I wouldn't like looking at it normally. It might be embarrassing. But it's different in the hospital.

'What's your name?' the doctor says to me.

'Jake.'

'Sit there, Jake, and watch the screen if you want to see the baby.'

Mum gasps when she squeezes something out of a tube on to her.

'Does it hurt?' I ask.

'No. Just cold.'

I'm not sure what's going to happen next, and Mum's right there next to me, so in case she's scared too, I take hold of her hand.

The doctor's running something over her stomach.

'Watch the screen,' she says again.

Darkness and light are moving about, and I can't tell what anything's supposed to be. It's like looking into a pool with water bubbling about.

'What's that round thing?' I say. 'Is that her head?'

The doctor looks up at me, surprised.

'Why do you think it's a girl?'

Mum laughs, and the image on the screen jumps.

'He says "she" all the time. He keeps doing it. Reckons he knows.'

The doctor smiles and turns back to the screen, but I've seen the look on her face.

I'm right. It is a girl.

I can see more of her now.

'That's an arm, see?' the doctor says.

150

My fingers have tightened round Mum's hand, and she squeezes them back.

It's like magic, seeing the baby, watching her move.

'Did you see me like this?' I ask Mum.

'Yes. Scared me stiff, I can tell you. That's when I knew it was for real.'

'Did anyone else see me?'

She snorts.

'Like who?'

'There's the left foot,' says the doctor.

I can't really make it out. I can't make anything much out, to be honest. It's all just shadows. But I don't need to look any more. I've seen her already, the little girl, with her dark hair and long pale face.

You won't have a dad either, I say to her in my head. Better not, though, when your dad's Steve.

The patterns of light and darkness move around on the screen. She's in there somewhere. The baby.

She'll have Mum and Grandma anyway. And my dad, a bit, sometimes. And she'll always have me. Always.

Kieran and I go around together all the time at school. We don't always go at the same time in the mornings, because it's not easy getting the timing right. Either he sleeps in and he's late, or I do, and I am.

But we always come home from school together. We get off the bus and walk over the railway bridge, and if a train's coming we can feel it rumble under our feet. Then we turn right and go down the lane.

He doesn't ask me about Dad, or anything, or about home, except to wonder if he can come round again next time Grandma cooks us a meal. I don't tell him much either. There's not a lot to tell.

Dad called me up all the time to start with. Once a day at least. More sometimes. We didn't always have a lot to talk about. He doesn't call so often now.

He's been back from Lancashire four times so far. He comes round to the flat straight off, and he and I go out and do stuff together. Sometimes I think I've known him all my life, and it feels like we're normal. A normal bit of family. Sometimes I get scared, in a panic inside, like I'm playing a part in a film and I'll get the lines wrong and be found out.

Mostly it's OK. Sometimes it's brilliant. Every now and then I feel upset, to be honest.

He did get me those rollerblades. For a surprise, he said. I didn't like that. I've had enough surprises to last me for ever. I don't care if I never get another.

I thought, If I can't do rollerblading he'll get fed up with me. He'll think I'm a wimp. He'll be disappointed, him having been a soldier and all.

Kieran grabbed them off me and had a go. It was a laugh. He doesn't mind looking daft and taking risks, falling about and crashing into things.

I tried a bit. I wobbled around in the lane, but I had to force myself. I could feel my stomach knotting up. I was frightened of falling over. I was afraid of pain.

Mum came past and saw me.

'Is that supposed to be fun?' she said. 'You look scared to death.'

'I am. I don't want to hurt myself.'

'Take them off,' she said. 'Give them here.'

I sat down on the kerb and handed them over to her.

'Men,' she said, and she sounded just like Grandma. 'They never think.'

I didn't see the rollerblades again. She must have had words with Dad because the next time he came down he said, 'Don't know what I was thinking of. Sorry, old son. Look, is there anything you want instead?'

'No,' I said. 'Not really.'

You don't have to buy me, I thought. I'm not for sale. I only want to be with you. Spend time together. Just get my confidence up so I know how to be your son.

I was coming home from school with Kieran today, same as usual, and when we passed my old hiding place, we looked at each other, I don't know why, then, without saying a word, we dived through the hole in the fence, me in the lead, Kieran behind.

No one had been there, I could tell. There was a quietness in the place and the grass and weeds had grown. Kieran and I went right on, through the space between the concrete blocks and out the other side, to the bank above the railway line.

'Did you come here often, before?' Kieran asked me. 'On your own?'

'Yes, loads of times,' I said.

Then I tried to reckon it up in my head. Why had I said that? I hadn't been here often. Hardly at all.

But things had happened in my secret place. I'd run here to be safe. I'd thought about my dream house. I'd nearly gone under a train, just down there, below the bank, and the baby had saved me. And then Kieran had come.

'I used to imagine things,' I said to Kieran, 'like planning my dream house in the future, where I'd really like to live.'

'I'm going to have a swimming pool in mine,' Kieran said, 'like in Beverly Hills. And a games room full of computers and stuff.'

He went on talking, about all the cars he'd have in his garage, and the football pitch out the back.

I tried to think about my dream house. I wanted to make up a different kind of place, to plan it, and be in it, and walk around in it in my head, like I used to with the old one.

There was a blank in my mind. I could only see the blue walls of my new-old bedroom, and the poster of the chimpanzee that Dad had given me, and the soft red cushions of the sofa in our sitting room.

'And I'd have a cinema in the basement,' Kieran was saying, 'with a popcorn machine so you could have as much as you liked without paying.'

I shut my eyes. All that remained of the old dream house were the silver and golden apples among the dark green leaves. They were twisting and turning, twisting and turning on their stems, shooting off sparks of light.

'It's boring here,' Kieran said. 'Let's go out into the lane and play football.'

'OK,' I said, and I followed him up, back between the blocks where the spider's web had been, and out into the lane.

The bushes closed over the hole in the fence once we'd gone through, and when I looked back I couldn't make out where my secret place had been.